# THE DOOR IN THE
# DRAGON'S THROAT

Other Books by Frank E. Peretti
*This Present Darkness*
*Piercing the Darkness*
*Tilly*

The Cooper Kids Adventure Series
*The Door in the Dragon's Throat*
*Escape from the Island of Aquarius*
*The Tombs of Anak*
*Trapped at the Bottom of the Sea*

# THE DOOR IN THE DRAGON'S THROAT

## Frank E. Peretti

CROSSWAY BOOKS • WHEATON, ILLINOIS
A DIVISION OF GOOD NEWS PUBLISHERS

*The Door in the Dragon's Throat.*

Copyright © 1985 by Frank E. Peretti.

Published by Crossway Books, a division of
Good News Publishers, Wheaton, Illinois 60187.

Cover illustration: © 1990 David Yorke

Printed in the United States of America

Library of Congress Catalog Card Number 85-70469

ISBN 0-89107-591-7

15   14   13   12   11   10   09   08   07   06   05   04   03   02
43   42   41   40   39   38   37   36   35   34   33

*To the kids at
Cedar Springs Camp,
1983*

# ONE

In the arid and strife-torn Middle East, land of Bible adventures, wars, camels, and kings, in the tiny, secluded, and landlocked nation of Nepur, a nation known for its strange customs and ancient mysteries, pompous President Al-Dallam, Chief Magistrate and Bearer of the Royal Sceptre, sat and fidgeted at his huge marble desk in the presidential palace.

An incredibly wealthy oil sheik, President Al-Dallam always wore a long, diamond-studded, purple robe, gold rings on his fingers, and a very impressive silk turban on his head. He loved being his country's president, he loved being rich, he loved being powerful. Right now, his huge desk was piled with important papers and business of state that needed his official attention, but he couldn't concentrate on any of those things. His mind was too flooded with thoughts of becoming even richer.

An excited knock on the big double doors to his office interrupted his daydreams, and a voice called excitedly, "Mr. President! My liege!"

Al-Dallam had been waiting all morning to hear that rough, raspy voice. "Gozan! Come in! Come in!"

The big doors burst open and in came Gozan, a bearded, rugged desert rat of a man. Al-Dallam imagined a small cloud of dust escorting his assistant into the office; Gozan always seemed to have a "common man" air about him. Gozan removed his big straw hat and made a hurried oops-I-almost-forgot bow.

"They have arrived!" Gozan reported excitedly.

The president rose from his desk, arms reaching heavenward in delight. "Ah, at last! Dr. Cooper's expedition is finally here! Now we will see what these Americans are capable of. Tell me—how many men did he bring?"

Gozan started counting his fingers as he watched faces in his mind. "Ummm . . . dah . . . ummm . . ."

The president was impatient. "Well? How many are in the expedition? He must have brought many—perhaps thirty, forty men?"

"Oh, no, my liege! Only his children and . . . three workers."

"Children?" The president was obviously unhappy, and that always made Gozan feel a little edgy.

Gozan tried to break the news gently. "Yes . . .

not *small* children, mind you . . . a young man and a young lady."

Al-Dallam slammed his fist on his desk and started pacing around the room, his purple robe flowing behind him like a peacock's tail.

"What kind of a fool is this Cooper?" the president fumed. "Children will only get in the way, get into trouble. I warned him of the great dangers."

"I . . . I also tried to tell him of the dangers, my liege, but he insists that he goes on no assignment without them. Apparently they are very well trained and can take care of themselves."

The president looked intently at Gozan with an expression he usually saved for decreeing death sentences. Gozan bowed, hoping to cool his superior down at least a little.

"Gozan, this is no task for children! It will take an army, not just four men and two . . . children!" Al-Dallam only shook his perplexed head. "They will all be killed the first day. The Dragon's Throat has no mercy!"

Gozan only shrugged, his eyes rolling. "Ehhh . . . it will not be the first time."

"But they must succeed!" the president bellowed. "Someday, somehow, someone must succeed!"

Gozan bowed again, and stayed bowed for a few moments. He knew that what he was about to say could be risky. "Mr. President, many have tried, and no one has succeeded. Not the German expedition with forty men and heavy machinery—

not the team from France who seemed so bold and confident. The United Nations exploration team couldn't even enter the Dragon's Throat before half of them were killed by scorpions and cobras. The Swiss expedition vowed never to return. You've sent letters to nations all over the world, but no one will dare to go near the Dragon's Throat! May my liege live forever, but why did you invite a mere scientist from America and his two young children? What made you think they could succeed where all the others have failed?"

The president spoke in a lowered voice. "I have heard reports about them. I have been told they are fearless. They are a peculiar kind of Christian."

Gozan snuffed through his nose and said, "Christians! Of what value is that? Others have claimed to be Christians . . ."

The president's eyebrows arched upward, crinkling his forehead. "Yes, but these people are different. They hold a very deep belief in their God, so much so that they derive some kind of special power from this deity. I don't understand their kind of religion, but they do not have the same fears as we do."

Gozan only laughed. "Ha! They've never tried to enter the Dragon's Throat. They've never tried to open the Door. They will learn to fear."

"But they must open the Door!" the president shouted in a sudden burst of anger. "Anything so impregnable, so fortified, so guarded by curses must contain incredible riches! I must have that treasure!"

"I could use some of that myself . . ."

"These Christians are perhaps our last hope. We must do all we can to make sure they succeed." The president looked at Gozan, and Gozan bowed again. "Gozan, I am making you responsible to help them. Give the American scientist every courtesy. Take him and his expedition to the Dragon's Throat, and escort them to the Door. Make sure they have whatever they need."

Gozan bowed hurriedly. "Yes, Mr. President! All that you instruct, I shall do . . ." Suddenly Al-Dallam's words struck home. "Did . . . did you say, 'escort them to the Door'?"

One of the president's eyebrows scrunched down over his eye. "Why, yes! You are a native Nepurian, an aide to the state and its president. You've been to the Dragon's Throat many times . . ."

"But never *inside* it!"

"You've accompanied many expeditions. You can go along with this one also, to make sure nothing goes wrong. With your experience and the many horrible failures you've witnessed, you can anticipate the problems before they arise. Your assistance will be invaluable."

Gozan's voice sounded like he had marbles in his throat. "But . . . surely you don't mean . . . me going with them . . . into the Dragon's Throat!"

Now the president's *other* eyebrow scrunched down. "I want to know, once and for all, just what it is that keeps happening down there. Most of all, I want them to succeed. I want you with them at all times, observing their efforts and making sure they do not fail. I want you to report back to me and let me know how they fare."

"My liege, live forever, but . . ."

"Are you opposing my will?"

Gozan bowed deeply, and answered quickly. "Your will is my will, my liege!"

The president smiled, his temper soothed. "Go! Meet them at the airport, and assist them for my benefit."

At the airport, consisting of one very small tar-surfaced runway in the middle of numerous wind-wisped sand dunes, Dr. Jake Cooper stood beside the large cargo plane, supervising the unloading of his cargo and surveying the surrounding land-scape. Dr. Cooper was handsome, rugged, tall, and strong, with blond hair. His intense expression and observant eyes indicated an inner commit-ment to tasks well done. He wore a hat, to shade his face from the hot desert sun, and work clothes that had already been through many challenging experiences.

"So this is Nepur," he said to himself, his eyes taking it all in, from one end of the horizon to the other. Nepur was mostly desert: sand dunes, low, bristly brush, hot rocks, scorpions, and snakes. The population consisted mostly of nomadic tribes, roaming the desert, herding sheep and goats, riding camels, and dodging cobras and thieves. In the distance was Zahidah, the capital city, where very rich oil sheiks lived in splendid mansions and very poor beggars lived in shacks, where one group hoarded all the wealth while the other group begged for the essentials of life.

Only a short distance away, a pit viper sunned himself on the hot airport apron, and the nearby rocks and grasses tingled with the countless tiny wiggles and scurries of scorpions, lizards, and tarantulas.

Nepur was not an inviting place.

Dr. Cooper's crew, unloading the cargo, was steadily building a sizable mound of crates, cases, and bags beside the plane. He continued to check off each item on his clipboard—checking, checking, and rechecking: tents, portable shelters, surveying instruments, climbing gear, tools, notebooks.

His son Jay, fourteen, was busy unloading his own pet items: seismometer, sonar, cases of dynamite, and plastic explosives. He was blond, not too tall, very firm in build. He'd followed his father around the world for most of his life, and it showed. If he wasn't already tough as leather, he soon would be.

Lila, thirteen, was years ahead of her age. Dr. Cooper's wife had been killed in a tomb cave-in in Egypt several years earlier, and Lila immediately began to occupy the empty space her mother had left behind. Archaeology was the only life any of them knew, and Lila took on the role of technician, organizer, and nurse with a real determination. At the moment she was rechecking her inventory of food and provisions and making a note to herself to lay in extra medical supplies. In a place like this, someone was bound to get hurt sooner or later.

What completed the gruesome picture welcoming them to Nepur was the strange sight at the rusting cyclone fence that bordered the airport. Directly opposite them, and for many, many yards along the fence in either direction, were crowds of people—women carrying half-clothed children, dirty, sweating oil workers, herders, beggars. A cross section of the population pressed against the fence like hungry cattle—nearly two hundred of them, staring, ever staring, not smiling or returning any greeting from the expedition party.

Lila asked very quietly, almost secretively, "What are they staring at?"

Jay volunteered, "I guess they've never seen Americans before."

"This place gives me the creeps," his sister concluded.

Dr. Cooper was not one to buckle under mere "creeps." "Curiosity-seekers, I imagine. Remember our arrival in that little village in Egypt? Any arrival of any airplane there was quite an occasion."

"Sure, Dad," said Jay, "but those people smiled. They were excited; they were even a nuisance. *These* people . . ."

Dr. Cooper looked again at the growing crowd outside the fence. Their faces were etched with a strange uncertainty, making him feel like he and his crew were lepers, freaks, an oddity.

With as subtle and nonthreatening a move as he could manage, he reached for his 357 Magnum and buckled the gunbelt around his waist.

"Everyone be in a state of caution. The Nepurians are an unusually superstitious people. Not even Islam has taken a very strong hold here. What I'm saying is, the culture of this people makes them entirely unpredictable."

Suddenly people began to stir and shout, scrambling to step aside as an old jeep came roaring through the airport gate and on toward the plane. The driver was rather wild looking, and his driving made the jeep seem more like a weapon than a vehicle.

Dr. Cooper recognized him. "That would be Gozan, our envoy from the capital."

Gozan roared up to the plane, hit the brakes, and left black streaks of rubber on the apron as the jeep screeched to a halt. He jumped out, flipped off his hat, and bowed low.

"Greetings to you all, and welcome to Nepur!"

Dr. Cooper introduced the eccentric character to his children and crew. "This is Gozan, special aide to the president of this great nation, the exalted and majestic ruler and Bearer of the Royal Sceptre, His Greatness Al-Dallam."

Jay, Lila, and the crew gave Gozan a cordial bow.

The aide grinned at Dr. Cooper. "You did that very well!"

Dr. Cooper returned the smile. "Thank you. You're looking well. I'd like to introduce my three technicians—Jeff Brannigan, Tom Foster, and Bill White." Gozan looked with appreciation at the three strong team members. "And my two children, Jay and Lila."

Gozan didn't look delighted over them at all. "Ehhh . . . yes, your children . . . we discussed them over the telephone, didn't we?"

"Yes," Dr. Cooper replied firmly, "and as you can see, I would not be dissuaded from bringing them."

"But they are so young . . ."

"And very indispensable to me," Dr. Cooper countered. "They are highly trained, highly responsible, and most of all they are my family."

Gozan finally shrugged and went on to other business. "We have reserved our best hotel rooms for you, your family, and your able crew, the very best the city of Zahidah has to offer."

Seeming to ignore the offer, Dr. Cooper queried, "How are conditions for camping at the site?"

Gozan drew back in disbelief. "You surely do not want to camp there, good doctor!"

"But we do, if possible. If we could be close to our work, we would save a great deal of time and expense."

"Nothing is worth camping near the Dragon's Throat, not at any time—and never, never at night!"

Dr. Cooper shifted his weight forward just a little. He always did that when someone needed some extra convincing. "We are equipped to do so, you understand. I'd like to see the site and then decide."

Gozan shook his head, his eyes wide and darting. "Believe me, this is not wise. The place is dangerous. It is cursed! We warned you of that in our letters."

"Yes, and I was fascinated to hear some of the folklore surrounding the Dragon's Throat. I found your old legends very informative, and I think the old superstitions might give us some clues as to what this strange cavern really is."

"You . . . you do not believe me, that the curse . . . that the dangers are real?"

"I didn't say that. But we serve a mighty God who is greater than any curse, and His Son died to free us from all curses. Local superstitions, true or not, could provide helpful clues of origin for me, but I'm not of a mind to be frightened by them. I'm here to explore the Dragon's Throat, and I'm here to discover once and for all what might be found behind this . . . this mysterious Door of yours."

Gozan took a deep breath, sighed, then replaced his hat with a flourish. "Ah, you are the confident one! I have vehicles ready to be loaded. If you wish to see the Dragon's Throat, to the Dragon's Throat we shall go." With a mocking grin he added, "But I will keep your hotel rooms available for you to flee to, brave doctor!"


Life moves slowly in countries like Nepur. The vehicles Gozan had "ready to be loaded" had yet to be finagled from the local army base. Furthermore, the two jeeps and two trucks they finally were able to borrow had already been through a few wars elsewhere in the world before they ended up in Nepur with battle scars, the creaks and rattles of old age, and no spare parts.

The military vehicles led a long caravan, squeaking and rumbling its way through the desert in the hot afternoon, kicking up the dust and looking like a single file of ants on the vast, barren landscape. The four vehicles loaned to the expedition were followed by no less than twenty others, ranging from automobiles to bicycles to mules. The curious staring crowd from the airport was following them, anxious to see what would happen at the Dragon's Throat.

Gozan drove the lead jeep, with Dr. Cooper riding beside him and Jay and Lila sitting in the back. Bill drove the other jeep, while Tom and Jeff drove the two trucks, now piled high with all the gear.

Dr. Cooper was amazed at the crowd of people following them.

"Talk travels fast in Zahidah," Gozan explained. "They heard you were coming. They are the idle, the do-nothings, the curious. They know why you are here, and they don't want to miss a thing."

"What do they think they'll miss?"

"Oh, some want to see the great treasure that will make our country—including them—very rich. The others . . . well, they have come to see you die."

Dr. Cooper was getting a little tired of such talk. "I don't intend to die," he stated matter-of-factly.

Gozan laughed uproariously, as if Dr. Cooper had told a joke. "You intend to tamper with the forbidden Door, doctor! That *always* brings death."

The caravan moved on, winding slowly through the dry, lifeless desert of sand, low brush, and towering rock formations. The ever-blowing wind, hot, dry, and sand-laden, howled mournfully among the rocks as scorpions scurried and snakes wrote repeating patterns in the sand. A few wild dogs ran across the road in front of the caravan, one carrying the dripping entrails of a recent kill.

The jeep climbed a long, gradual rise, then neared the top. For a moment, all the passengers could see over the hood was the deep blue, cloudless sky. As the front of the jeep dropped—too suddenly, it seemed—they gazed onto a sweeping panorama of the vast desert valley below. Gozan skidded the jeep to a stop in the gritty sand, and the whole caravan came to a halt behind them.

"There it is, brave doctor."

Dr. Cooper stood up in the jeep and looked over the top of the dirty windshield. His eyes narrowed with great interest, and he pushed the brim of his hat back, a subtle gesture of amazement. Jay and Lila jumped out of the jeep and came up beside him to have a better look.

It was an eerie sight. Below them stretched a wide, desolate valley bordered on either side by low, sunbaked hills and rocky crags. The floor of the valley was peppered with low, bristly desert brush and scattered rocks. But in the very center of the valley, looking very unnatural, was a wide, circular area at least a quarter of a mile across in which nothing—absolutely nothing—lived or existed. The ground inside the circle was ashen, a glistening, salty white, as if a meteor had hit or an explosion had blown everything within the circle to white, powdery dust. Furthermore, in the very center of this huge circle, the ground fell away into a deep hole, a dark, gaping cavern that looked like a sinister funnel, a bottomless whirlpool carved in rock and sand.

"The Dragon's Throat," Gozan said simply.

"A meteor crater?" Dr. Cooper asked.

"No. Every expedition has thought that at first, but there was no explosion, no impact. It is a deep cavern in the middle of nowhere, with no cause or origin, here for as long as history can remember. It is a pit that seems to drink in the rest of the earth, a home for death."

"Another legend, I suppose?"

"As you know, we have many legends, doctor. You can take your pick. The local nomadic tribes make this site the home of their many gods, a sacred place no one can approach under penalty of death for themselves and an eternal curse for their families. Some say it is the very throat through which the earth feeds, and many sacrifices have been cast into it.

"There is a story too about a young shepherd who lived long ago. He was seeking a stray goat and found it dead on the rim of the forbidden circle. He entered the circle himself to find out what had happened to his goat. Perhaps he entered the Dragon's Throat itself. No one knows. But he was never the same again, and spent the rest of his days roaming the desert and living like an animal, wailing and howling in the hills around this valley."

Dr. Cooper surveyed the craggy rocks and hills carefully. With just a little imagination they could become a perfectly terrifying place for a legend to be born in the ghostly hours of the night.

"You haven't mentioned the legend that brought me here," Dr. Cooper said. "The legend about the great star that used to sail across the heavens, that plundered the earth and hid his treasure deep within it."

"Yes . . . yes, I recall that one. It has not been as popular, probably because it does not strike so much terror into the hearer's heart."

"Probably. And it could be the only one with a germ of truth in it. You see, Nepur is not that far from the location of ancient Babylon, the ancient kingdom of Nimrod mentioned in the Bible—Genesis chapter 10."

"I have not read it."

"Nimrod was a powerful ruler, regarded by his people as a deity. He plundered the earth and no doubt amassed an incredible treasure. If the legend and my interpretation of it are true, there could at least be a wealth of knowledge hidden here, new information on the early history of man right after the days of Noah."

Gozan leaned back in his seat and shook his head slightly. "In the service of your God again, good doctor?"

"Absolutely," Dr. Cooper answered, peering down at the strange pit through a pair of binoculars. "I make it my business to search out the remains of civilizations the Bible talks about. The information I uncover is invaluable to Bible scholars."

"*If* you manage to open the Door. Perhaps this Nimrod you speak of *was* a deity, and perhaps it is his curse that protects the Door now."

"Where is this Door you keep referring to?"

"Oh . . . like we told you, somewhere down inside the Dragon's Throat. I have never seen it. Some claim to have seen something. Few have lived to tell us *anything*."

Dr. Cooper turned to Jay and Lila, who were sharing another pair of binoculars. "Any comments, you two?"

Jay looked at his father, then at Gozan. "Our God is greater," he said with a shrug.

Dr. Cooper smiled. "My thoughts exactly."

"We will see," muttered Gozan.

"But first we'll have to find this Door of yours, won't we?"

Gozan took the hint and put the jeep into gear. Jay and Lila jumped back in and away they went, down the hill and into the valley. The rest of the caravan started moving sluggishly along after them, like so many links in a dragging chain.

The wind behaved differently in the valley, moving in wide arcs, like water swirling in a large tub. Dust-devils spun and swayed across the desert floor, and mirages flickered on the sand like distant tinsel. The passing vehicles spooked the desert floor into life as lizards, snakes, and huge crawling insects darted in all directions.

Gozan brought the jeep to a stop about fifty feet from the edge of the lifeless circle.

"If you don't mind, I'd like to wait here," he said, turning off the engine.

The caravan rumbled down the hill and began to fan out behind them like animals coming to a watering hole. Dr. Cooper remained in the jeep and watched them all, not knowing whether to be irritated or simply amazed. He'd never seen anything quite like this. Bill, Jeff, and Tom brought the jeep and two trucks alongside, but they didn't get out and wouldn't until they saw Dr. Cooper do so.

Dr. Cooper waited until the caravan—the cars, trucks, bicycles, sweating workers, crying children, trudging mothers, and mumbling beggars—was finally settled and quiet, and that took some ten to fifteen minutes. When the noise finally died down and things got quiet, he sat very still and listened for several more minutes.

For the first time, in the absence of any machinery noise, they could hear the deep, guttural howl of the wind moving across the Dragon's Throat. The cavern rang with an eerie resonance like a huge bottle; the sound was quite mournful.

From the big truck right next to them, Tom hollered, "What do you think, Doc?"

Dr. Cooper was pretty casual when he said, "I have a viper here. I'm waiting for him to make up his mind."

Jay and Lila leaned out of the jeep to look. Sure enough, right beneath their father's door lay a snake, looking up at them, his neck moving to and fro in graceful arcs, his tongue flicking the air.

"What shoes do you have on?" Dr. Cooper asked them.

Jay lifted his foot, as did Lila. Their boots were thick-soled, tough-leathered hiking gear.

"Got another one over here," Tom said, pointing to a slithering, iridescent band moving around the tires.

"But not one inside the circle . . ." Dr. Cooper mused.

"So let's drive in there," Tom suggested.

"No!" Gozan blurted. "No further!"

Dr. Cooper watched as the viper finally decided to turn away and take his fangs elsewhere.

"Okay, let's do it," he said, "but watch where you step."

They carefully climbed out of their vehicles and deliberately made their way over the rocks. Gozan sat in the jeep, watching their every move, as did the hundreds behind them, sitting in or on their conveyances, parked along the perimeter of the circle, watching and waiting.

Dr. Cooper, Jay, Lila, and the three crewmen made their way to the very edge of the circle. Dr. Cooper stooped down for a closer look.

"Not even insects," he said. "Nothing enters the circle. Jeff and Tom, bring the trucks up here. Lila, prepare the Geiger counter."

Dr. Cooper took the Geiger counter from Lila and held the sensors close to the edge of the circle. No reading.

Jeff was making soil tests. "No caustic substances. Pretty neutral stuff, just plain sand, high silica content."

"Perfectly normal, in other words," said Dr. Cooper. "Jay, get out the walkie-talkies. I'm going to send you and Lila around the perimeter to look for geophysical indications, cracks, fissures, ashfall, anything that could give us a clue."

Jay was already in motion.

Dr. Cooper suddenly noticed Gozan joining the group at the circle's edge.

"Well, hello there," said Dr. Cooper.

Gozan shrugged. "You are still alive, and I do have my orders from the president."

Dr. Cooper smiled. "So this is some kind of oddity. It doesn't fit any known pattern yet. Not a volcano, not a steam vent . . ."

Jay was ready with the walkie-talkies.

"Head around the perimeter," Dr. Cooper instructed, "but don't step inside. Just watch your step, and report anything that could be a clue. We'll keep in touch."

Jay and Lila started around the rim of the circle, enduring the stares of the many observers as they passed by them.

Gozan was smirking a little. "So, doctor, you are not so quick to be brave after all!"

"One reason I'm still alive today is because I don't take chances. Well, not too many anyway." He spoke into the walkie-talkie. "Jay and Lila, how's it going?"

"Nothing to report," came the answer.

Dr. Cooper picked up a stone and threw it into the circle just to see if anything would happen.

Gozan laughed at him. "Doctor, the Dragon's Throat is taboo to foolish men, not to stones."

Dr. Cooper poked his toe into the circle,

scraped some of the sand as a little test, and then, without hesitation, took several full steps inside. Many cries and gasps were heard among the observers. He checked the Geiger counter; there was still no reading. He walked a little further into the circle. Looking back toward the crowd, he could see their frightened eyes growing wide and their mouths hanging open.

He spoke into his walkie-talkie. "Jay and Lila, report."

The two teenagers were still picking and choosing their way along. There had been no more snakes, at least that they could see, but Lila had accidentally crushed the tail off a scorpion, and Jay had pegged rocks at two lizards. It wasn't much of a report to give their father.

They now came up against an outcropping of very large rocks that came right to the edge of the circle. They would have to go around them, working their way outward.

Jay replied into his walkie-talkie, "Nothing unusual, Dad. We're about halfway around the circle. Can you see us?"

"Yes," came their father's answer.

"We'll have to duck behind these big rocks for a while. See you in a bit."

A stiff, intermittent wind was kicking up on this side of the circle. The big rocks provided shelter from it, but clouds of dust were moving across the desert floor, temporarily obscuring their path.

"Should've brought some goggles," Lila muttered, wiping and blinking her eyes.

Suddenly she felt Jay's hand grab her arm.

She froze, knowing it meant some kind of danger. She searched the ground for a threatening insect or reptile, but her eyes were drawn quickly to the same sight that had startled Jay.

In a small pocket between two large rocks above them, the dust had dropped away during a brief lull in the wind, and there, as if appearing out of nowhere, stood a ghostly figure of a man— old, gray, with a long scraggly beard and dressed in a tattered robe. His face was dark, leathery, and wrinkled; his eyes were intense. He held a crooked staff in his hand, which he pointed at them.

Jay whispered to Lila, "Do you see what I see?"

"I think so."

Jay shouted to the strange apparition, "Are you for us or against us?" The question sounded scriptural, and that gave Jay a little courage.

The old man spoke in a voice that sounded like a rockslide as he pointed the crooked staff at them. "Americans—Christians—heed my warning! Do not go near the Dragon's Throat! Do not open the Door!"

Lila piped up, "Who are you?"

"Do not open the Door! Only unspeakable evil and death await you!"

The stranger turned to leave.

"Hey," Jay shouted, "wait a minute!"

But the wind carried a cloud of dust across the opening in the rocks, rather like a curtain being drawn across an exiting actor. When the dust had passed, the old man was gone.

Now they had something to report. Jay reached for his walkie-talkie.

"Dad . . ."

Lila took a wrong step as she tried to see where the old man could have gone. Her foot kicked a rock aside, and what happened next was like a sudden explosion of horror.

HISSSSS!!!

They both froze in fear. A silvery shaft shot out from the rocks and curled up into a lethal question mark right in front of them.

Dr. Cooper returned Jay's call. "Yeah, come in, Jay." Jay didn't answer. "Jay, did you call me?" Silence.

Jay held the walkie-talkie close to his face, but the words wouldn't come. Lila huddled near him. Both of them were motionless. A long, narrow shadow like a swaying palm tree moved from side to side at their feet—the shadow of the huge king cobra now rearing its head and hooded throat right in front of them. They were pinned against the rocks and had become like rocks themselves. Only their eyes moved, watching the snake's every motion. The cobra kept making a hideous hawking sound from deep in its throat, its white mouth gaping and its fangs glistening with venom.

"Jay? Are you there?" squawked the walkie-talkie. "Come in."

The black eyes of the cobra seemed to bore holes right through them. It studied them, hissed at them, flicked out its long, red tongue.

The seconds turned into hours as sweat drew streaks in the dust on their faces and they stared into the face of death.

# TWO

"Jay!" the walkie-talkie squawked again. "Jay, come in! Can you hear me?"

Jay could feel the pounding of his heart clear to his fingertips as he very carefully and slowly pressed the talk button. He hoped his voice would be loud enough for his father to hear even though it was choked with terror. "Dad . . . we've disturbed a cobra . . . it has us cornered."

Gozan looked away for only a moment, but when he looked again where Dr. Cooper had been standing, he saw only a Geiger counter lying on its side where it had been dropped in the sand.

"Lord God," Dr. Cooper prayed, "grant to me the lives of my two children!"

He ran with remarkable speed across the bleak and lifeless circle, carefully looking for the location where he last saw his kids. "Halfway around . . . halfway around . . . near that outcropping of rocks . . . straight across . . ." His feet pounded the white sand as he shot forward in a dead run.

Jay and Lila remained frozen and the cobra seemed to relax a little, its reared head settling inch by inch to the ground, though its cold black eyes kept them in its sights. Lila could feel her tense muscles starting to ache and throb. Sweat was pouring down Jay's back.

Dr. Cooper ran past the very edge of the Dragon's Throat just as the wind resonated through the deep shaft with an angry howl. A terrible fear shot through his every nerve, and he could feel the adrenalin coursing through him. He kept running, sprung into motion by the energy that terror brings. He had no time to wonder where the fear had come from; he attributed it only to the plight of his children.

The snake's head was only a few inches from the sand when a pebble fell. The head came up again, and the same hawking sound spewed out of the snake's gaping white mouth.

Suddenly the snake's head disappeared in a spurt of blood. The loud crack of Dr. Cooper's 357 reached the kids' ears as the twitching neck fell to the dust writhing in a roll of death.

Jay and Lila still didn't move. The snake was dead, but they couldn't quite believe it.

"Are you all right?" came Dr. Cooper's call.

They moved just enough to look toward the voice and saw Dr. Cooper coming toward them, still brandishing his gun. They relaxed, looked all around to be sure it was safe to move, and then scrambled out of their trap.

Lila ran to her father's side, and he put his arm around her. She burst into tears and let out a few loud sobs.

"It's okay, honey, it's okay," he comforted her.

"I know," she said between gulps of air. "I just have to get it out."

"How are you?" he asked Jay.

"I . . . I want to sit down for a minute," Jay confessed.

"Let's get into the circle. It's open and safe there."

They stepped across the forbidden line and walked across the white sand until they felt a safe distance from the sinister desert. They sat down for a moment. The sand was hot under them.

"Nice shot, Dad," Jay said, his voice still a little shaky.

"Keep practicing yourself."

"Oh yeah!"

"Did you find anything else besides an angry cobra?"

"A scorpion and two lizards. Nothing geological, though. Are we sure this whole thing isn't man-made?"

"We're not too sure about anything just yet. How's it going, Lila?"

"I'm . . . I'm very terrified."

"So am I," Jay said.

"And so am I," said their father. That seemed a little odd to them; Dr. Cooper was rarely frightened of anything. "I don't know. Feelings are so subjective, it's hard to determine what's causing them . . ."

"I hate to say this," Lila observed, "but I almost feel safer back there in cobra-land."

Dr. Cooper looked over toward the big rocks which they had just left and then surveyed the strange, barren circle all around them. He then looked for an especially long time in the direction of the yawning pit.

"I think," he said at last, "I'm afraid of that cavern over there."

Jay and Lila were troubled to hear that. Jay asked, "What do you mean, Dad?"

Dr. Cooper frowned and shook his head. "Jay, that's what bothers me. I don't really have a good reason. I can't quite figure out what exactly would evoke this kind of fear in us."

Jay finally remembered the strange encounter with the old man. "Dad, we saw someone right before we stumbled onto that cobra . . ."

Dr. Cooper listened with great interest as Jay told him the whole story. "He didn't say who he was?"

"No. He just appeared and disappeared, and gave us that warning."

Dr. Cooper thought about that for a while and then said, "This whole thing is beginning to look like a lot more than a routine archaeological dig. Why all the interest in this cavern? And what would make hundreds of people all drive clear out here, so sure they'll see us die? The superstition around here is incredible!"

Jay had to admit, "I don't like the sound or the looks of this whole situation."

Lila added, "It makes me wonder what we're really getting into."

"We're about to get into that cavern," replied Dr. Cooper. "Let's go have a look at it."

They forced themselves to walk, fear or no fear, across the featureless circle to the very center, where the Dragon's Throat awaited them and greeted them with a dull, moaning howl. The wind swept along, carrying the fine sand in slithering, floating wisps until it came to the chasm where it swirled about like a whirlpool and rang the walls of the pit like some huge, inverted bell. The howling sound was quite loud where the three explorers were now standing, and the many different tones, the low rumblings, the shrill whistles, the wails and moans of countless chambers and orifices in the rocky walls of the cavern could be heard clearly.

The three stood at the edge, peering downward at the steep and rocky walls that disappeared into the darkness far below. They couldn't see the bottom at all. The walls of the Dragon's Throat nearest them were sheer vertical cliffs, but the walls across the pit from them were more sloped and gradual, and most likely climbable. They thought they could even see what looked like a primitive trail. They walked around to the other side to have a closer look.

Jay kept looking down into the pit and shaking his head. "Boy, it really is just like looking down the throat of a dragon."

"And the dragon is howling at us," Lila added.

Dr. Cooper was a little more scientific in his musings. "I make it to be at least a hundred and fifty feet across the opening . . . no way to tell how deep. But the shaft descends at an angle, not vertically, and that might make it easier to climb down. It isn't limestone . . . doesn't follow the usual formation patterns of a natural cavern. A person could say it was a volcanic venthole except for the total lack of ashfall, volcanic rock, *anything.*"

Lila peered down into the deep hole and said, "There's something evil about it. I just get that feeling."

Dr. Cooper didn't really disagree, but merely drew Jay and Lila close and said, "Now would be a good time to review. Who are we?"

Jay and Lila didn't answer right away. They were too mesmerized by the cavern.

"C'mon, now," Dr. Cooper prodded, "who are we?"

"We're God's children," they finally answered.

"And even though we may walk through the valley of the shadow of death . . ."

"We will fear no evil."

Jay added, "Greater is He who is in us than he who is in the world."

Dr. Cooper gave them both a loving squeeze. "All right, listen—caution and prudence are always a priority in this work, but unfounded fears shouldn't be allowed to enter our minds. Listen, folks, if we don't trust God, how can we expect others to? He'll protect us—He always has. We have a job to do, so let's get at it."

Back where the others were waiting, Gozan was full of questions. "You . . . you were gone so long. I was afraid the Dragon's Throat had swallowed you up. Some have said the Dragon's Throat is alive and feeds on those who venture too close."

"I guess it had no appetite today," Dr. Cooper muttered as he prepared a list of tasks and preparations.

"But . . . but did you feel it? Did you feel the evil, the curse?"

Dr. Cooper looked up from his list with narrowed eyes and said firmly, "The cavern is a natural formation in the crust of the earth. As for this curse, the evil you speak of is nothing more than your own fears playing tricks on you. Now I'd like you to get some gear from the equipment truck. You're going down with us."

Gozan backed away, holding his palms toward the doctor, shaking his head, his eyes widening. "No, no, not me, good doctor!"

"Listen, we are still very much alive and intend to stay that way. We'll protect you, all right? It's part of our agreement with your government that we bring along a native observer, and I believe that's you. You can report back to the president whatever we find."

"But . . . but what about the curse?"

"We serve a Lord and Savior who is greater than all curses. We're not afraid."

"No god is greater than the curse of the Dragon's Throat. I have seen what it can do!"

"*Our* God is greater. You'll see."

Jeff, Bill, and Tom already had all the vehicles moved out onto the clear sand and away from hidden creatures. They were now arranging all the climbing and cave gear: special climbing boots, spikes, ropes, lights. Dr. Cooper organized the exploring party, which included all six members of the expedition plus Gozan, frightened though he was.

Within half an hour, the expedition's vehicles were driven right to the edge of the Dragon's Throat. Gozan even brought his jeep, although he whimpered and protested the entire distance.

"Let's do it," said Dr. Cooper, and the seven of them started toward the side of the pit with the gradual descent.

"May the gods protect me . . ." whined Gozan. "May the spirits of my ancestors protect me."

Just as they reached the point of descent, a sickening, chilling wail rose up from the depths.

"The dragon growls at us!" Gozan cried.

Dr. Cooper paused at the top, and the entire party—except Gozan—instinctively removed their hats.

Dr. Cooper prayed out loud, "Lord God above, we thank You for bringing us to this, a new adventure and opportunity for discovery. We pray for success and for the furtherance of Your kingdom through the knowledge we may gain here. We plead now the shed blood of Jesus to cover us and protect us from danger. Amen."

"Amen!" said Jay and Lila.

"Amen!" said the three crewmen.

"Let me go back!" said Gozan.

Dr. Cooper took the first steps into the cavern, letting himself down very carefully onto a rocky ledge just below. Bill let down the doctor's safety rope foot by foot, keeping it taut.

Soon all the members of the party were making their way down into the Dragon's Throat, all linked together by safety ropes and each trying to step in the same place as the one who went before. Every rock was tested before any weight was put on it. Some rocks failed the test and crumbled away, plunging into the cavern and disappearing into the deep blackness before a distant clatter could be heard as they smashed into the unseen floor far below.

"Well," said Jay, "at least we know this thing has a bottom."

"I'll be disappointed if that's all there is down there," said Dr. Cooper.

They worked their way like cautious mountain goats back and forth, rock to rock, ledge to ledge, moving steadily downward for over an hour. For quite a while there was a swirling wind current whipping about in the shaft, but when they climbed below that the air grew still and musty.

Dr. Cooper shined his light downward, and they could see that the huge shaft was beginning to take a turn sideways. The steep walls opposite them were moving away, while the walls they were climbing on grew more gradual. They were evidently approaching the bottom. High above them, the entrance to the Dragon's Throat had become a small circle of light surrounded by black walls and darkness. It was very much like climbing down a huge, deep well.

The climbing became easier and more gradual toward the bottom, and eventually they weren't really climbing at all, but just leaping from rock to rock until they came to the bottom of the cavern. The floor was sandy, slightly damp, and quite easy to walk on.

Gozan shined his light around the cavern, the beam shaking a bit because of his obvious nervousness.

The cavern suddenly reverberated with the aide's scream. Six other lights shined immediately in the same direction as Gozan's and illuminated a rotted skeleton with gaping jaws and unseeing eye sockets, lying prostrate on the floor, the limbs curled up tightly.

"The curse!" cried Gozan. "We're all going to die, just like him!"

Dr. Cooper grabbed Gozan and tried to contain the man's violent emotions. "Calm down! Do you hear me? Calm down! We're right here, and we're still alive, can't you see that?"

Gozan calmed himself, but his breath was still very unsteady and panting.

"That's better. Now, can you tell us who this might be?"

Gozan shined his light on the dead figure, taking a painful look for details. "Yes . . . yes, there on the backpack. That insignia. He was the lost member of the Swiss expedition. Five went down into the Dragon's Throat . . . only four came back out. They all fled in utter panic, and they had no interest in returning for . . . this one."

Jeff shined his light above them, examining the walls and ledges. "Do you think he may have fallen from up there? That would be quite a distance."

Dr. Cooper, unconvinced, took a closer look. "I don't think he died from a fall. Look at the position of the body—all curled up, the arms protecting the head. Something terrified him."

Jay whispered, "Dad, can you hear something?"

The group fell silent, listening intently.

Gozan asked nervously, "What is it?"

"Shhh!" they all replied.

They stood silent, holding their breath. They couldn't tell if they were hearing something or feeling it, it was so very deep, so very quiet, so all-pervading. From somewhere came a very low vibration, a distant, barely discernible rumble. It seemed to be coming from all around them. Some sensed it coming up through the floor.

Dr. Cooper was fascinated. "Air currents maybe. The entire cavern is remarkably resonant."

Gozan had his own theory. "Spirits, all around us! The ghosts of hell!"

Dr. Cooper asked the group, "Is anyone paying any attention to him?"

No answer.

"Good. All right, let's stow these ropes for now. Same order, single-file. Let's press on."

There was no other way to go but down. They followed the slope of the sandy floor along a vast tunnel that penetrated deep into the earth. Along the way they found various items of gear dropped by the fleeing Swiss party. Here and there were several large boulders that had fallen from the ceiling—not a very comforting thought.

As they moved along step by step through the slowly expanding tunnel, that strange rumbling sound grew more loud until there was no mistaking it. It was there, all right, a real sound. They could hear it vibrating in the resonant stone walls; they could feel it in their feet.

They kept pressing ahead. The sound of every footstep, every breath, every rustle, seemed to flit and dart about the cavern in a myriad of little undying echoes before it finally faded away. Except for the sweeping beams of flashlights, there was only total, inky darkness.

It was the echoes, those bouncing, undying sounds, that first gave them the hint that the tunnel was emptying into a huge room. The tight, oceanlike sound of the air in the tunnel, laden with the echoing sounds of the exploration party, began to slowly ebb as the echoes weakened and went further before bouncing back. The tight enclosure was widening, the ceiling was rising, the walls were curving outward.

Dr. Cooper paused, and the party came up to stand quietly beside him. He shined his light high above, and the beam, powerful though it was, had weakened to a dull yellow wash of light by the time it reached the ceiling, hundreds of feet above them. The others shined their lights in all directions and found that they had come to the entrance of a room that had to be at least the size of a sports stadium. The air was perfectly still and silent; the cavern was cold, musty, and dark.

And the rumbling sound continued. Whatever was making it had to be in this huge room.

"We'll divide into two parties," Dr. Cooper instructed. "Gozan, Jeff, and Lila, come with me. The rest of you follow Bill. We'll move along the opposite walls of the room and meet on the other side of it. Keep in radio communication at all times."

The two groups started out, one going left, the other going right. They moved carefully along the walls of the cavern, their light beams playing on the rocks, sweeping across the lofty ceiling, and casting eerie, dancing shadows that swayed, grew, and shrank, leaped and fell. The sounds of their footsteps and the quiet clanking of their backpacks and gear were muffled in the vast expanse of dead air.

Dr. Cooper moved in and out of the fallen rocks and jagged formations, followed by Lila, who had Gozan more or less in tow. Then came strong and burly Jeff, who brought up the rear. Across the way they could see the other party's dancing beams of light, appearing as distant searchlights.

"Bill, how's it going?" Dr. Cooper asked on his walkie-talkie.

"Fine as frog's hair. Nothing unusual," came the answer.

"Good enough. We can see your lights and we're . . ."

Dr. Cooper didn't finish his statement. His feet were feeling more than that mysterious rumble. The ground now seemed to be quivering. Gozan felt it too and began to whimper.

"Look for cover," Dr. Cooper instructed.

They all ducked under outcroppings of rock or pinned themselves tightly against the walls as the tremors increased. The earth was shaking under their feet; it felt like a giant freight train was passing only a few feet away, but there was no thunderous sound, only the plinking and plopping of pebbles here and there and the hissing of falling sand from the ceiling.

"Bill, how are you?" Dr. Cooper wanted to know.

"Sitting it out, Doc," came Bill's answer.

And then, as if the train had passed, the quaking ebbed away. All was silent again.

"Everybody okay?" Dr. Cooper asked.

"Fine," said Lila.

"Yeah, okay," said Jeff.

"I . . . I am still alive," said Gozan.

Bill reported the same thing over the walkie-talkie.

Dr. Cooper shined his light above, checking the large rock formations on the walls and ceilings. "I really don't want any surprise packages falling on me."

They continued their trek through the big room, but it wasn't long before Dr. Cooper's walkie-talkie squawked with Bill's excited voice, "Doc, I think we've found something!"

"Let's see your lights," said Dr. Cooper, and

immediately the lights from the other group began to wave excitedly across the walls and ceiling not too far ahead. "I see you. Hang on, we're coming!"

He and the others quickened their pace, choosing their steps carefully but hurriedly, making their way through the rocks and obstacles, the beams of their lights piercing the darkness frantically.

Finally they met the others. Bill, Tom, and Jay were shaking with excitement.

Jay shined his light forward, toward the very end of the room. "Take a look at this, Dad!"

The other beams of light all followed Jay's, and Dr. Cooper looked on the sight with amazement. He felt his heart would stop as he stood there silently, his face etched with awe and fascination. Then he felt Gozan crouching, hiding behind him, and Gozan was the first to say anything.

"The . . . the Door!" he gasped.

Dr. Cooper spoke up. "Jay, shine your light at the top. Bill, shine your light at the middle. Let's get our lighting spread out so we can see the whole thing."

The light beams flooded the new discovery, making it more visible—and even more incredible.

There, in the distant wall of the huge room, was what looked like a massive, towering door. It could have been stone, it could have been iron; from here it was impossible to tell. The lower half was covered with fallen rocks from some ancient cave-in, but the upper half was clearly visible, reaching a height of some eighty feet and a width of at least thirty. It was a dirty, dusty gray and appeared to have been there since time began, cut into that towering wall and sealed so tightly it almost seemed a part of the wall itself.

Dr. Cooper was totally awestruck, as were the others.

Gozan could only tremble and mutter, "The legend is true! The legend of the Door is true!"

Dr. Cooper turned to Gozan and asked, "So you've honestly never seen this Door before?"

Gozan shook his head, unable to take his eyes off the Door. "No, never. I've only heard the legends."

"Well, someone must have seen it . . ."

Gozan laughed a nervous laugh and said, "Many, good doctor, but none have lived to tell about it." Then he added with a gulp, "And neither will we!"

Dr. Cooper guided Gozan over to Jeff, who knew from Dr. Cooper's glance that he was to keep control of this poor scared fellow. Then Dr. Cooper approached the Door, stepping onto the pile of rubble that covered the Door's bottom half.

"What kind of treasure could be hidden behind a door so large?" he wondered aloud.

No one had time to answer. Suddenly, as if in response to Dr. Cooper's approach, the earth began to quiver and shake again, but this time it was no small tremor. It occurred abruptly and with great force, and several of the party, including Gozan, were knocked to the ground. Pebbles began to rain down like hail, and a deep rumbling from the awakened earth grew louder and louder. The floor of the cavern heaved to and fro, throwing the explorers back and forth until they finally had to hang desperately onto rocks, cracks—any handhold they could use to steady themselves. Jay huddled under a ledge of rock and could see the boulders on the cavern floor beginning to sway with the force of the quake. To everyone's horror, the ceiling began to shower rocks and boulders down on them; huge chunks came down with heavy thuds and dug into the floor. There were very few places to hide.

Where is Dad? Jay wondered, shining his light toward where he'd last seen his father. No sign of him. Too much dust.

There he was, still standing on that pile of rubble, desperately trying to keep from falling as the rocks beneath his feet began to shift under him.

"Dad!" Jay cried out as he started to run to help his father.

Only a split second passed before Jay felt himself propelled sideways by a huge body. It was Jeff, knocking him down in a flying tackle and then dragging him along.

BOOM! A boulder the size of a large automobile punched a crater in the floor where Jay had just been standing.

Jeff and Jay scrambled to safety in another small nook in the wall of the cavern.

Jay frantically looked toward the Door and the pile of rubble for any glimpse of his father. He was still there, trying to get somewhere safe, struggling to maintain his footing, trying to avoid the rocks that were rolling and careening past him.

But Jay could also see a telltale stream of dust and pebbles falling in a narrow stream from somewhere above his father. He shined his light up, following the dust until he could see the earth and rock beginning to crumble away around an immense chunk of rock in the ceiling. The massive boulder was shaking loose, and it was right above his father!

Jay screamed with all he had in him, "Dad, look out!"

But the roar and rumbling of the quake and the pounding of the falling rocks were too loud and drowned out Jay's desperate cries. Dr. Cooper could not hear the warning and remained where he was.

Then, with a loud crackling and a snap, the huge boulder began to shift and tear loose, and then it dropped.

# THREE

During a moment that passed in slow motion, an instant of inexpressible horror, Jay gave out one long, wide-mouthed, helpless scream that no one could hear.

"JEEEEESUUUUUSSSS!"

At that moment the earth gave a forceful, sudden lurch, throwing Jay back into Jeff's big body. The two of them slammed against the cavern wall as if thrown there, and they could no longer see Dr. Cooper.

With a slow, lazy tumble, the boulder nosed into the pile of rubble with a sickening, very final *crunch,* and then eased over on its side and lay there like some huge dead thing.

The earthquake subsided immediately. The roar of the earth gave way to the settling sounds of the rocks, and that sound finally gave way to the gentler, rainlike sound of plinking, plunking, hopping pebbles coming to rest everywhere.

The crew, particularly Jay and Lila, couldn't wait to come out of hiding. Beams of light formed conical shafts through the dust and haze, swinging wildly about as the explorers tried to find each other.

Jay was just about to holler for his father when all of them heard Dr. Cooper's commanding voice booming down from behind the killer boulder. "Any injuries in the party? Report."

"This is Bill. I'm okay."

"Jeff here. Jay and I are all right."

Jay had his own questions. "Dad, I want to know about *you!* Are you all right? Where are you?"

Dr. Cooper responded with another question. "Lila, are you all right?"

Lila was getting cross with her father, purely out of worry. "Dad, honestly! Tell us how you are!"

Then they saw a beam of light wiggling about from behind the boulder, and finally there was Dr. Cooper's head poking up into view just above it.

"Dad!" both teenagers cried with delight and relief. They clambered toward him.

"Careful!" he cautioned. "The rocks are newly fallen; they're loose!"

"Are you all right, Dr. Cooper?" Bill asked.

The kids could see a trickle of blood on Dr. Cooper's forehead. He had discovered it himself also and proceeded to dab it with his handkerchief.

"I'm all right," Dr. Cooper finally reported to

everyone. "A slight cut on the forehead, but nothing major. I took a spill back here."

Then came Gozan's hoarse, hysterical voice from somewhere in the dark. "I saw it! I saw it! The boulder was about to crush the good doctor, but then the earth responded to young Jay's call and knocked the doctor out of the way!"

"That is basically right," Dr. Cooper conceded. "That last big shake knocked me over, and just in time. I'd say this cut on my head is a fair trade for my life."

By now Jay and Lila were hugging him, and he seemed more concerned for their well-being than his own.

Gozan, his face blackened by dust and sweat, finally emerged from his hiding place, his eyes big and round.

"Your God controls the powers of the earth, yes?" he said.

Dr. Cooper held Jay and Lila close as he answered boldly, "Gozan, our God controls everything. He is the Creator of all things."

"Maybe," Gozan dared to venture, "maybe He is stronger than the curse that guards the Door?"

Dr. Cooper found his hat, but Lila took it from him as she said, "Our God is more powerful than any curse!" Then she told her father, "No hat until I take a good look at your head!"

The three of them climbed down from the pile of rubble to join the others as Gozan continued to marvel.

"All the other expeditions would have been

dead or would have fled in terror by now. Your God has protected you. He has protected all of us."

"That is correct," said Dr. Cooper as they all clustered together on the cavern floor. "And we are going to thank Him for that right now."

Hats came off, arms went around shoulders, heads bowed, and Dr. Cooper gave a heartfelt prayer of thanksgiving for the Lord's protection. Gozan only stood there, still wide-eyed, impressed by the strange faith of this group and very, very impressed by the towering, ominous Door that seemed to be watching them, aware of their presence.

So they found what they had come for, whatever that was. But first things had to come first. Tents, shelters, and temporary storage buildings were quickly set up at the edge of the Dragon's Throat, and the hotel rooms in Zahidah were no longer kept reserved. Jeff managed to wheel and deal some old lumber from a slightly shady supplier in the city, and for the next few days the crew worked on a very effective string of ladders and stairways down the steep sides of the cavern to the sandy floor far below. A powerful gas generator provided electricity for not only the camp, but also for strong floodlights all along the cavern corridor to the big room where the Door still waited to be challenged.

Throughout this time, whenever the sound of

hammers, saws, or voices would cease for a moment, that strange rumbling sound could still be heard. Interestingly, it always grew louder and a little higher in pitch whenever someone got close to the Door; and not only that, but even the earth seemed to get nervous, shaking and quivering.

Every day Gozan would hurry in his old jeep to Zahidah and let President Al-Dallam know how things were going.

One such day, a week after the expedition first arrived, Gozan enjoyed a rest on the president's soft couch and drank a large mug of herbal tea as he shared the latest update with the president.

"Perhaps you were right, my liege," he said after a loud slurp of tea. "These explorers, these Christians, could be different indeed. They are still there, and they are still alive."

The president was trying to be hopeful, but he couldn't help pacing about the room and looking out his window toward the forbidding desert. "They have not yet *succeeded*, Gozan!"

"But, my liege, they are still alive. Maybe their God will help them to open the Door as well."

At that comment, the president couldn't help enjoying at least one moment of glee. "Yes . . . yes, perhaps the great Door will finally be opened, and the fabulous wealth hidden there will be mine . . . uh . . . will belong to the people of Nepur. Such wealth will make us as great as the other states belonging to our people. Ha! Let them have their oil! We will welcome the nations of the world to come and look upon our vast, priceless treasures."

"Provided the curse of the Door does not destroy our whole nation . . ." Gozan mused, swirling his tea leaves.

"But these Christians . . . ! They may be the answer. They may be able to break any curse."

"Much evil has been caused already, and only because we have dared to enter the Dragon's Throat . . ." Gozan couldn't help muttering. "What evil do you suppose could be unleashed if the Door itself should be opened at last?"

This very question was still haunting Gozan the next day when he accompanied Dr. Cooper to the base of the huge Door. The floodlights were installed, the Door was brilliantly illuminated, and Dr. Cooper was now ready to make another attempt to approach it.

"Good doctor," Gozan pleaded, "the . . . the earth shakes every time anyone gets near the Door. The Door knows we are here."

Dr. Cooper casually inventoried the tools in his toolbag, handed the bag to Gozan, and said, "Gozan, one of these days I'm going to have to give you a basic lesson in exactly what causes earthquakes. Believe me, people don't cause them. Now let's take a look."

They climbed up the pile of rubble—one step, one boulder, one shaky rock at a time, carefully picking each foot rest. The size of the Door made it seem close, but it still took a considerable climb to get up to it. Now flooded with light, it looked even more immense, even more sinister. The recent earthquake had knocked some of the thick dust off, revealing a very rough, aged, bronzelike surface underneath. It must certainly weigh hundreds of tons.

Gozan suddenly squeaked in fright.

"Not again!" Dr. Cooper moaned.

The cavern was beginning to shake once more. Rumblings and deep moans echoed all around. Rocks quivered and rolled down from the walls; dust from the cavern floor began to rise like a thickening carpet of fog.

"What did I tell you, doctor!" Gozan said with a quivering voice. "What did I tell you! The Door! It knows we are here!"

"Oh, stop it!" Dr. Cooper ordered.

The shaking stopped—just like that.

As far as Gozan was concerned, even this sudden silence was scary. "The earth! It heard! It obeyed you!"

Dr. Cooper only shook his head. "Come on, let's go."

At last, feeling like they had just conquered a treacherous mountain, the two of them reached their goal. They reached the Door, which towered above them and made them feel like mice.

Dr. Cooper touched the dirty, dusty surface.

"Feels a little warm," he observed.

"Never have I seen such a thing!"

"Shhh! Listen."

The two of them stood there very silent. "I think . . . we may have found the source of that rumble . . ."

They leaned toward the Door and listened. It was unmistakable. From somewhere behind the monstrous Door, deep within the earth, came that strange sound. From here it was better defined, with more complex overtones: a very low droning, with many different whirrings, hummings, and higher pitched rushing sounds.

"It sounds like a horrible beehive," Gozan observed.

"For lack of a better description," said Dr. Cooper, his ear close to the Door's surface. "Could be air currents . . . perhaps geothermal expansion and contraction . . . maybe nothing more than a swarm of bats. I've never heard anything like it before, but it does reverbrate throughout the cavern and most certainly originates here."

"It seems much quieter now. Perhaps the Door is afraid of you."

Dr. Cooper ignored the comment. "Let me have the brush there."

Gozan handed him the brush, and Dr. Cooper began to carefully clean away the dust and sediment from the surface of the Door.

"Yes . . ." he muttered thoughtfully as he worked. "Bronze. Ancient hammered bronze. But what kind of primitive technology could have formed anything so huge?"

Gozan pointed excitedly. "What . . . what's that?"

"What we're after," Dr. Cooper replied. "Here. Scrape that dirt away right there. Use that little claw tool. That's right. Now let me brush it off. Aha . . ."

"Writing!"

"Yes, we're uncovering an inscription of some kind. An unusual writing style, but it could be a form of Babylonian. It does fit that kind of construction. Maybe I can make it out."

The two of them worked quickly, their excitement growing. Dr. Cooper continued to carefully brush away the dirt as the inscription was slowly unveiled.

"All right!" he said suddenly. "Look—that symbol right there, right there in the corner. That means star."

Immediately Gozan thought of the legend. "The star . . . from heaven, you suppose?"

Dr. Cooper did give Gozan a glance of acknowledgement this time, then kept scraping and brushing. "Yes . . . yes, it is! Here! This symbol here means heaven, the upper atmosphere, the sky. . ."

Gozan could only exclaim, "Star, heaven!"

The inscription continued to be revealed under Dr. Cooper's rapidly working brush. "Yes . . . and here's the symbol for . . . falling, flying, being hurled. Yes! Here's the whole sentence: 'The star that flew through heaven . . .' "

"The legend!" Gozan said, his eyes bulging. "The legend is true!"

"Nimrod . . ." Dr. Cooper couldn't help wondering out loud, "Could this be the lost treasure of Nimrod . . . ?"

Gozan loved that word. "Treasure!"

"Look. There's more to the inscription. Key. Here's the word for key. 'The star that flew through heaven . . . uh . . . holds . . . has brought . . . no, *will bring* the key, and all . . . will be released.' "

"The treasure of Nimrod!"

"We can't be sure yet, but it makes sense. Nimrod, the ancient ruler of Babylon, conquered the world, hid his treasure here, and apparently was the sole possessor of the key to this door."

"The treasure of Nimrod! Dr. Cooper, we are rich!"

Dr. Cooper was already thinking ahead. "We'll have to get this pile of rubble away from the Door. Go tell Jeff and Bill to bring the blasting equipment."

Gozan hesitated, looking this way and that.

"What's wrong?" Dr. Cooper asked.

Gozan fidgeted, looked downward, then smiled a very strange smile Dr. Cooper had never seen before. "Good doctor, wait. Take . . . just a moment to think about this. *We*, doctor . . . *we* are the ones who have found the treasure. It is ours."

Dr. Cooper knew this was going to be a conversation he would not enjoy and had no desire to get into. "Gozan, we don't know for sure whether there is a treasure, and even if there was, it would belong to the Republic of Nepur, not to you or to me."

Gozan threw his head back and had a really good laugh. "Oh, Doctor Cooper, you can be honest with me. Surely you were not going to let the nation of Nepur have all the treasure and not keep any for yourself. No man is that foolish."

"I believe I asked you to go after the blasting equipment."

But Gozan was in earnest. He would have made a good salesman. "Doctor, doctor, listen! Only you, with the help of your God, can even approach the Door and live. Only you and I know what lies behind it. We need not tell anyone else, and no one else will even dare to enter the Dragon's Throat. The treasure can be ours!"

Dr. Cooper's voice was cold and threatening. "Perhaps I should just tell President Al-Dallam that—"

That did the trick. Gozan held his hands up in surrender and blurted, "Oh, no! No! No need to do that! I will go after Jeff and Bill . . . and the blasting equipment."

"And tell Jay and Lila to come quickly with the sonar."

"Yes, yes . . ." Gozan said as he clambered down the rocks. "But . . . think about it, doctor! Think about it!"

"I'll do no such thing!" Dr. Cooper muttered angrily.

Jay, high on the pile of rubble and to one side of the Door, was pounding against the walls with a huge sledgehammer. On the opposite side of the Door, Lila pressed a special electronic sensor against the stone wall of the cavern. Down below, on the cavern floor, Dr. Cooper monitored the reading on a special sonar device, listening for the echoes of Jay's hammering coming back through the recess behind the Door and watching the pattern of lines forming on the little video screen. He was making faces, turning the dials, and looking puzzled.

"Uhhh . . . Jay, move in a little closer. Lila, you move in too."

They followed his directions.

"Okay, try it again."

Jay pounded the wall several times, and Lila kept the sensor against the opposite wall.

Dr. Cooper leaned back and shook his head, staring with perplexity at the machine. "I'll have to have Bill check this machine over. I don't think it's working."

"What's the matter with it?" Jay asked.

Dr. Cooper scratched his head and said, 'Well, according to this readout I'm getting, there's nothing but infinite space behind the Door. The sound just travels off into infinity and never comes back."

Lila objected, "Well there has to be something back there—walls or *something!*"

Dr. Cooper only shook his head. "Not a thing."

"Here you go, Doc!" came Bill's gruff voice.

Bill and Jeff arrived from topside, carrying a case of powerful plastic explosives and a detonator.

"Okay, great," said Dr. Cooper, packing up his machine. "Let's get this rubble out of the way."

"Just leave it to us, Dr. Cooper!" said Jeff.

"Oh, we'll leave, all right!" Jay said.


Soon the entire party stood at the bottom of the long stairway—far below the cavern's entrance and far away from the big room where the explosives had been set.

Bill held the small electrical detonator in his hand.

"I like this part," he said. "We'll make those boulders dance like popcorn!"

"Everybody ready?" asked Dr. Cooper.

No one said no, so Bill threw the switch.

And yes, one could say it sounded like popcorn all popping at once—if the kernels were the size of houses and weighed several tons each and the popper were a monstrous stadium. Everyone put his hands over his ears, but they could still hear the boulders bounding and pounding against the walls and ceiling of the big room like wild Ping-Pong balls. They all kept their widened eyes glued on the corridor, expecting one of those cute little Ping-Pong balls to come bouncing out at them any moment.

All they saw, however, was smoke and dust, which lazily drifted up the corridor several minutes after the crash and clatter of the explosion had ceased.

"Well, maybe you did all right, Bill," Dr. Cooper said a little teasingly.

"No maybe about it, Doc," Bill replied. "You go back in there and you'll find one bare Door, clean as a whistle."

"It'll take a while for all that dust to settle. Jay, now would be a good time for you to break out your seismometer up on top. Place some sensors around the circle up there so we can get a better idea where these quakes are coming from. Gozan, why don't you go with him? You could use some fresh air."

Jay loved working with the seismometer. He loved working with any gadget actually. This particular device was a favorite of his, though, and he'd worked with it many times before. It was a fascinating machine. It could register a man's footsteps miles away. Should another earthquake hit, the machine would be able to tell them where it was originating, how severe it was, and, most important, what was causing it.

Gozan assisted Jay as best he could, following Jay around the circle and planting the various sensors evenly around the circumference. He was more of a hindrance than a help, however, when his mind started running in the wrong gear again.

"So . . . ," he began, with that same strange smile on his face, "what do you think of our great discovery?"

Jay was honest about it. "I think it's terrific. I can't wait to see what's really behind that Door."

Gozan laughed a cackling sort of laugh and said, "Why, a treasure, of course. The lost treasure of Nimrod." Then his voice lowered, and he moved in closer to Jay to say, "You know, if you wanted, you could be a very rich young man."

But Jay only smiled patiently. "*If* there *was* a treasure, and *if* it belonged to me in the first place."

Gozan stayed close to Jay as they walked along. Jay just kept trying to think about where to plant the next sensor, even though Gozan kept rattling away in his ear.

"You . . . you have helped your father find it," Gozan said gushingly, "and I don't know about you, but . . . I have always believed that . . . he who finds is he who owns."

"Finders keepers, in other words," said Jay, planting a sensor and rechecking its spacing from the others.

Gozan did not have sensors on his mind. "Yes! Finders keepers, yes, just as you say!"

Down below, in the big room, Dr. Cooper, Bill, Jeff, Tom, and Lila were inspecting the lower half of the Door, now "clean as a whistle" as Bill had promised, and easily accessbile. Now the Door was twice as tall and made one feel twice as small to be standing next to it. Dr. Cooper carefully ran his fingers along the seams of the Door and probed the very minute crack with a fine, sharp tool.

"A perfect fit, to begin with," he reported. "Perfectly snug and tightly sealed. It's been this way for centuries."

Tom was always the heavy equipment man. "I could take a good drill to it."

"Let's try it," Dr. Cooper agreed.

Meanwhile, Jay's patience with the blabbering Gozan was getting very thin.

Gozan just kept pecking away at him. "It would be so simple to carry the treasure away, out of the country. You have the plane, you have the vehicles . . ."

"Gozan!" Jay finally snapped. "You're asking

me to take something that doesn't belong to me. That's stealing, sneaking, plotting, and betraying, and I won't do it!"

"But . . . but why not? What is right for you is right!"

Jay's mouth dropped open at that. "What's right for *me?* Is that all you can possibly think about, just what *you* want? Listen, you don't go against God's laws! When you do, you only hurt yourself."

"But doesn't your God want you to be happy? Doesn't He want your father to be happy?"

"God wants us to do our job, to do what He wants us to do. That's where real happiness comes from!"

"Jay, I am only trying to help you out!"

Jay was really mad by now. "No, actually you're trying to ruin this project, and I'd much rather you just keep quiet and help me set out these sensors. Is that too much to ask?"

The roar of Tom's drill filled the big room with a cascade of echoes. He was sweating profusely, leaning on that drill and grinding away near the base of the Door. Everyone nearby could smell something burning, and before long the drill bit simply snapped off.

"Nuts!" Tom exclaimed angrily. "Don't touch that bit. It's hot."

"How's it look?" asked Dr. Cooper.

Tom inspected the spot where he'd been drilling. "Sorry, Doc, but it isn't going to work. Look, I haven't made a scratch, and I used my biggest drill."

Dr. Cooper straightened up and tilted his hat back a little. "Well, that sure isn't bronze then. What kind of metal could be so tough that you can't even get a drill through it? Ancient Babylon had no metals like that."

Bill asked, "So what now, Doc?"

Dr. Cooper could see the plastic explosives already in Bill's hands. "All right, give it a try. Set your explosives around the edges of the Door, in the seams. We'll see if we can't loosen that door enough to get it open."

"Just watch!" said Bill. "Hey, I forgot the detonators . . ."

"I'm on my way," volunteered Lila.


Jay and Gozan had finished setting out the sensors, and now they huddled near the real core of the apparatus, the seismometer itself, which was sitting on a stand near the Dragon's Throat at the center of the circle. Jay adjusted the controls and made some preliminary test readings.

Gozan watched with fascination. "How does this work?"

Jay explained as he worked. "Well, you see all these needles here, drawing the lines on the paper as it rolls by? Each one is tuned to one of the remote sensors, and if a sensor picks up any tremors in the earth, the needle will start to wiggle and make a wavy line. We examine the pattern of the wave, and that tells us what's going on out there."

"But . . . but some of the lines are wiggling now."

Jay knew it and was trying to fine-tune the machine to get a more accurate reading. "Yeah . . . nothing big, not yet at least. But there is some kind of activity down there, and it does seem to be centered near the Door . . ."

Lila had just reached the top of the stairs, puffing a bit, and was going toward the supply shed when she could feel a very familiar and un-welcome quivering under her feet.

Jay and Gozan kept watching the seismom-eter. Jay's eyes were glued to the wavy lines on the moving paper.

"Okay" he said, "very heavy tremors now on the machine . . . a kind of rippling going on . . ."

"Yes!" Gozan said excitedly. "I can feel them. The earth is angry."

"Sensors four . . . five . . . eight . . . ten . . . there goes nine. The shock waves are rippling out-ward . . . from the Door!"

"The Door! The Door! Someone is tampering with it!"

Lila kept walking, even though she was stag-gering from the shaking. What a life, she thought, when one eventually got *used* to earthquakes! She staggered to the left, and she staggered to the right. Her tracks in the sand looked like a drunk-ard had come by, she thought as she headed for the supply shed. When she finally got there, the whole shed was quivering and creaking, and the door rattled in its frame. She reached for the door handle.

The door flew open, and Lila found herself sprawling on the ground, stunned by the blow. What had hit her? The wind? The earthquake? What made the door—?

She froze in terror, for towering over her, his white hair blowing wildly in the breeze, his eyes big and piercing, stood that mysterious old man with the crooked staff and the leathery face! He was even more frightening up close like this, and Lila found that a scream had become jammed somewhere in her throat. This was like a night-mare. She wanted to run, but couldn't; she wanted to get up, but the ground shook so hard she couldn't do that either.

The old man grabbed her up violently and with powerful strides began to run across the bar-ren circle, his hot breath chugging into her face, his grip strong as steel.

Lila kicked, struggled, tried to loosen the old man's grip, tried to remember her self-defense tricks. But this was a strange creature carrying her, with crazed eyes and incredible speed.

And the scream still wouldn't come.

# FOUR

Jay and Gozan were watching the seismometer and had no idea of what was happening behind their backs.

Lila, however, had finally been able to release a desperate scream. Jay and Gozan spun around at the sound of it, and saw the old ghostly figure quickly shrinking into the distance, carrying his kicking victim. They broke into a dead run, knowing the distance would be difficult to make up.

The old man looked back and then slowed to a stop. Now what? Lila thought. She planned a good jab at his eyes if he made one false move.

But he set her down very gently with the muttered words, "You'll be safe here," and then raced away like a frightened animal.

Jay and Gozan reached her in just a few moments.

"Are you all right?" Jay asked.

The answer was just forming on Lila's lips

when all three of them were blinded by an incredible flash of orange light and then deafened by a tremendous explosion. They dropped to the sand, covering their heads and each other.

The supply shed blossomed in a ball of fire as shreds and splinters of material were propelled in all directions. A huge cloud of smoke billowed skyward. The sound of the blast slammed into the surrounding mountains and rocky crags, where it was broken into hundreds of separate sounds that rebounded back across the valley, slapping the air and the desert floor with echoes upon echoes and explosions upon explosions. Boards and splinters began to return to earth in a hazardous shower; shreds of paper fluttered down like scorched snowflakes.

Jay took a cautious look. The worst was over. Gozan and Lila raised themselves up. Gozan was the first to speak or rather to shout.

"The Shaman! The Shaman of the Desert! It was him! Are you all right, Miss Lila?"

"Did he hurt you?" Jay demanded.

Lila answered, "No, I guess not. How are you?"

"Don't worry about me." Jay turned to Gozan. "Gozan, what did you say?"

Gozan was trembling. "It was the Shaman of the Desert. He blew up the supply shed."

"You know who that was?"

Gozan's eyes were big; his body was trembling. "The Shaman! A magician! Immortal! He is part of the legend surrounding the Door. It is said he guards it, and that he has great power to destroy anyone who dares to violate the ancient curse."

Lila skeptically responded, "Oh, brother! We should have known better than to ask you."

"It is *true,* Miss Lila. You were in terrible danger."

"Some magician!" said Jay. "He's more like a petty saboteur, it seems to me. It's a good thing we have more explosives in the other shed."

Gozan shook his head, pounded the ground in despair, and moaned his lament. "We are doomed! We have aroused the wrath of the Shaman! Everything is against us! Our lives are marked now for horrible death!"

"I . . . I don't think so," said Lila. "I don't think so at all."

"Why not?" Jay asked.

"I don't think he meant to kidnap me. Did you see the way he came to this point and then set me down? He said something about my being safe here. I think he was just trying to get me away from the explosion. He was trying to keep me from being hurt."

Jay could see the sense in that, but too much of it still didn't make sense at all. "He warned us not to open the Door. Then he blew up our supplies, obviously to keep us from succeeding. Just what is he up to anyway?"

"Well, I notice the earthquake has stopped."

Jay chuckled a bit. "And I didn't even notice when. Sis, I never thought you could be more exciting than an earthquake."

"Well, don't expect me to do it for you again."

Gozan looked up from his pit of despair and muttered, "The earth only shook when *he* was here!"

Lila was ready to change the subject. "Dad's waiting for some detonators," she said, getting up.

"Yeah," Jay agreed. "Let's get on with this project. Whew! Wait till he sees this mess up here!"

Dr. Cooper listened to the account Jay and Lila told him and put up with Gozan's colorful embellishments, and then stood there in a very thoughtful mood while the whole crew waited to hear his next order. He scowled, dug in the sand with his toe, walked back and forth with his hands gesturing to his silent thoughts, and then stared at the Door for the longest time, like a gladiator staring down an opponent, like a general sizing up an enemy's army. He stared, and he thought, and they all waited. He drew a long, deep breath.

"The answer to all this lies behind that Door," he said finally. He then looked at Bill, who was still holding his wonderful explosives, and said, "Open it."

Bill smiled very confidently and set right to work, directing all the crew in placing the explosives in just a certain way around the seams of the Door. They used ladders and ropes to reach as high as they could up the Door's sides, carefully packing the explosives into the cracks. Bill inspected every placement, every person's work, every quantity of the stuff. Everything had to be just right. The work took hours.

Then they all gathered, not at the base of the stairs, but at the very top, on the ground, at the edge of the Dragon's Throat. Bill would use a radio detonator this time and a series of special relays. No one needed to be anywhere near the blast.

"Well sir," Bill said, looking at them all, "if this doesn't open it, nothing will. I just hope we don't bring down the whole cavern."

"I trust you, Bill," said Dr. Cooper.

"Thank you," Bill said rather grimly. He was unusually serious about this particular blast. "Hang on to your hats!"

He pressed the switch. Jay, who had his eye on the seismometer, immediately saw the needles go off the paper. Everyone could feel the rumble of the blast under his feet. The Dragon's Throat began to rumble and growl, and then issued a tremendous, angry roar as smoke, dust, and gas billowed out of the shaft like the eruption of a volcano. They all scrambled back from the edge of the cavern as the cloud poured out of the hole and drifted, black and ugly, across the desert floor.

"Hoowee!" Bill exclaimed. "That was pretty!"

"What happened down below?" Dr. Cooper wondered. "I'll be surprised if you didn't disintegrate it."

"Trust me," said Bill.

To be safe, they waited until the following day to reenter the cavern. As they entered the big room, they could see that Bill's plans had worked quite well. The room itself had escaped any kind of wholesale devastation; all the power of the blast had been concentrated against the far wall.

They hurried to the far end of the room, groping along in the semidarkness. Tom finally found the switch to turn on the lights at that end. The floodlights came on, the far wall was illuminated, and they all stood there dumbfounded, their mouths open, their eyes gawking.

"Shew!" was all Dr. Cooper could say.

"I . . . I just don't believe it!" said Bill.

The Door was blasted clean and now shone like burnished bronze; the walls all around it had been seared clean by the blast. But the Door remained firmly shut. It hadn't budged a bit.

They all went in for a closer look. The entire Door was exposed now, every inch if it; the dirt and dust of the centuries was gone. The seams were clean, and much of the rocky outcroppings nearby had been blasted to powder.

But the Door was still sealed shut. It towered over them defiantly, like the mysterious entrance to some fantastic giant's castle.

Jay, like the others, was awed and amazed. The Door was actually beautiful, shining in the lights as it now did. His eyes moved up the seams of the Door, examined once more the mysterious inscription halfway up, and then noticed something no one had noticed before.

"Dad," he said, "look up there."

"Where?"

"See there? Right above the inscription. What's that?"

Dr. Cooper looked, as did the others. Tom chuckled a little.

Dr. Cooper said softly, "Don't tell me!"

Lila ventured to say what they all were thinking: "It looks like some kind of keyhole."

Dr. Cooper was almost laughing himself as he said, "That's exactly what it looks like. That last blast finally uncovered it."

"The legend!" Gozan blurted. "The inscription, doctor!"

" 'The star that flew through heaven will bring the key and all will be released,' " Dr. Cooper recited. "Great! So somewhere there's a key to open this thing?"

Bill, chomping on a wad of gum as he stood beside Dr. Cooper, concluded, "Well, seeing how my explosives can't open it, a key might help."

"It's scaffold time," Dr. Cooper ordered. "Let's get a platform up there so we can get a closer look at that keyhole, or whatever it is. Can anybody pick a lock?"

There were no takers.

They did set to work, however, and began constructing a scaffold to gain access to the keyhole.

Lila organized some of the tools. After the blast, fine dust had become a problem, and she found she had to clean several of the adjustable wrenches to unjam them. She reached into her pocket for a handkerchief, but encountered a little scrap of paper instead.

She unfolded it and found some curious writing on it. She scowled and squinted as she read it, and then called to Jay.

"Jay! Look at this!"

Jay finished driving a nail and then joined her. "What on earth . . . ?"

"That strange old man must have slipped it into my pocket when he set me down yesterday. Can you make out the words?"

The two of them tilted the paper toward the lights to get a better look. The writing was hard to read, but between the two of them they finally deciphered, "Please meet me . . . 1107 . . . Street of the Scorpion . . . tomorrow at sunset. I will explain."

"Hooboy!" said Lila. "That's tonight."

Jay called, "Dad, I think you'd better have a look at this."

The sun was a huge, red ball of fire just touching the distant sand-duned horizon as Dr. Cooper drove the jeep into Zahidah. Jay and Lila were looking over a crude map of the city, trying to find the Street of the Scorpion.

"Oh, oh," said Lila, "here it is. On the east side of the city."

"That's what I was afraid of," said Dr. Cooper. "That's the least inviting part of Zahidah. It's a maze of tight little streets, an anthill of impoverished, desperate people. It's crawling with thieves, criminals, occultists, sorcerers . . ."

"Shamans?" Jay asked.

"At least one, I suspect."

"What if it's a trap?"

"We'll have to take that chance. I understand

that the local militia never go near that area, partially because there are too many passages and places for a criminal to hide, and partially out of fear and superstition. I think that old character knows that full well too."

"This is sounding worse all the time," Jay said.

"Well, whoever he is, if he really wanted to kill us he could have done it very easily before."

Lila added, "And I still think he was trying to save my life."

"But he blew up our supply shed," Jay reminded her.

"So," observed Dr. Cooper, "he wants to stop us, not kill us. In this part of the world, there has to be a reason."

They entered the city and made a turn toward the east side. Almost immediately, as if crossing a border, they drove from a city of regal splendor into a stinking sea of squalor and filth. They drove past closely packed shanties and bungalows made of wood scraps, cardboard, old car fenders, anything. Wood smoke hung in the air like thick, nostril-burning smog; scavenging dogs scrambled about in motley packs; ragged, half-naked children played in the dirt. The streets were little more than tight spaces between rows and rows of old stone slums with rat-infested gutters and dirty human beings with blank expressions and vacant stares.

They entered a maze of tight streets that wound down, around, through, and under old buildings of stone and brick, wood and mud, lumber and scrap. The night and neighborhood were getting darker and darker, and Jay tried to read the map with the aid of a flashlight. Following Jay's directions, Dr. Cooper turned left, then right, then squeezed the jeep under a very low footbridge, then drove through an old courtyard past a broken fountain oozing green slime. From there they wound and twisted deeper and deeper into the maze. All the dull stone walls of the dismal dwellings were beginning to look the same.

Dr. Cooper pulled the jeep to a stop beside an old man with a mangy, garbage-fed dog. He jabbered to the man in two or three languages until he finally got some response and a pointed finger to show them the way. They continued on.

All the light of the dying day was gone by the time Dr. Cooper brought the jeep to a halt at what appeared to be a dead end. Stone walls towered all around them like the walls of a canyon—or a prison. There were several narrow passageways leading out of the very small square, but none wide enough for a vehicle. Dr. Cooper shined his flashlight here and there, and finally spotted the odd, foreign squiggles on a faded sign.

"Street of the Scorpion," he said.

"Oh, terrific!" Lila said with foreboding.

Dr. Cooper checked his gun. "Okay, let's go."

They got out of the jeep and went to the narrow little passageway which had somehow earned the name of a street and peered into the blackness. From here it looked like a dangerous, dark, drippy cavern, with stone walls rising straight up into the blackness of the sky and a dank, slimy pavement that glistened in the beams of their lights.

"Stay together," said Dr. Cooper.

They started into the passageway, one step at a time, looking all around, trying to be as silent as they could. The thick, wet air seemed to carry the sound of a snicker or a fiendish laugh. They could hear invisible rats skittering just ahead of their footsteps. Mmrroowww! A black cat jumped aside, and the kids leaped several feet.

Dull, yellow candles burned in the windows they passed, and dark shadows moved about silently in the rooms. Occasionally they would catch a glance from a set of yellow eyes that seemed to float in the blackness without a face. The eyes would stare for a moment, and then blink out with disinterest.

"Watch your step," Dr. Cooper whispered, and they all stepped carefully around a narrow, deep hole in the middle of the passageway—a hole that reeked of sewage and starved carcasses.

They heard the snicker again. It sounded diabolical.

"How much further do we have to go?" Lila whispered as she followed right behind Jay.

"I don't know," Jay answered softly. "I can't make out any of these numbers."

"Well, I just hope—"

There was a muffled cry, a scraping of feet, the rustle of clothing, and then nothing. Jay reached behind himself and swung his hand to and fro, but felt nothing.

"Lila?" No answer. "*Lila?*"

Dr. Cooper heard a muffled cry from Jay, some kicking, some more scraping. He spun around, and the beam of his light caught a foot just slipping through a very low doorway.

"*Jay!*"

He bolted for the door, burst through it, and found himself in what felt like a mole's tunnel. The ceiling was low, and he had to crouch. He looked this way and that and saw one door down at the end just swinging shut. He dashed for it, but it clicked shut before he could get there. It was locked.

The 357 snapped into action, and fire flashed from the barrel as the tunnel rang with the shots. The lock became scrap, and Dr. Cooper's boot took care of the door itself. He leaped through the doorway and found himself looking down four different passageways which wound in four different directions. He listened carefully. From down one passageway there came the slightest little shuffle. He dashed after it, found another door, went through it, came upon a dead end, doubled back, tried another passageway, found nothing, tried a third, found a door, went through it . . . and found himself right back where he'd started.

He stood still. He looked. He listened.

He heard that devilish snicker again, along with the distant cry of a cat and the skittering of rats' feet in the deep darkness. He heard and felt the steady, stinking, dripping of decay borne on the thick, wet air.

He could hear no other sound.

# FIVE

President Al-Dallam was sitting comfortably on a very soft couch in his private parlor, munching on raisins and nuts and enjoying a satellite broadcast of a soccer game on his wide-screen television, when the big, ornate doors burst open and Dr. Cooper came in like an army invasion.

"Mr. President!" the American yelled.

The president, very startled, was immediately on his feet, his eyes full of surprise and questions, his fat cheek full of raisins.

"What is the meaning of this?" he demanded.

A very imposing guard stepped in behind Dr. Cooper and started to grab him, but Dr. Cooper plunged his elbow into the guard's stomach and was obviously prepared to further defend himself.

"Let him be," the president ordered. The guard sheepishly left the room. "Doctor, this is most improper!"

"Mr. President, I don't have time for decorum. My children have been kidnapped."

"What?"

"We were keeping an appointment in the city, and someone grabbed them and carried them off. I need your assistance! Your police! Your militia!"

The president seemed very slow to see anything serious about any of this. "Kidnapped?"

"Do you know the meaning of the word?" Dr. Cooper queried sarcastically.

That irritated Al-Dallam. "Of course I know the meaning . . ."

"Then I need your help. We've no time to lose."

But the president only rolled his eyes in disgust and sank back down onto his couch.

"Kidnapped," he moaned impatiently. "Oh, those children! I knew they would be trouble. Doctor, I invited you to this country to open the mysterious Door, and you only bring me trouble. Children who get themselves abducted!"

Dr. Cooper couldn't believe what he was hearing. He stepped around the big couch and faced the president.

"Is that Door all you ever think about? Where is your human heart, man? My children are in danger! I demand that you do something! I'll offer a reward!"

At that statement there was a gruff snorting and snoring, and then the slurred question, "A . . . reward?"

Over in the corner of the room Gozan's burly head appeared from behind the couch he'd been sleeping on. The mention of a reward had awakened him.

Dr. Cooper meant what he said. "Yes, I'll offer a reward to whoever finds my kids."

"How much?" Gozan asked, his teeth glistening with a greedy smile.

"You can name your price."

The president jumped to his feet again, his anger rising. "*My* price is that you get the Door open! That is why you were brought here!"

Dr. Cooper could not be stared down or intimidated, not even by this haughty potentate. "No more work proceeds on the Door until my children are found safe." He narrowed his eyes and added, "Period."

The president's gaze dropped, then slowly drifted over to where Gozan was sitting. "Gozan, find his children."

Gozan rose from the couch with all the grace of a slug and said, "Certainly, certainly. For a *price.*"

"Your *life*, perhaps?" the president said coldly.

It was amazing how Gozan could become so efficient so suddenly. He stepped forward very briskly and asked, "Where were the children last seen, good doctor?"

"The Street of the Scorpion on the east side of the city."

If Dr. Cooper had stabbed Gozan through the heart, he would have gotten the same reaction.

"The . . . Street of the Scorpion!" Gozan gasped.

The president was also very disturbed. "What were you doing *there?*"

Gozan drummed his fingers against each other as he said, "The Shaman! It had to be the Shaman!"

"That's right," said Dr. Cooper.

The president's face was red with anger. "So he has come out of hiding again, and this is his mischief?"

Gozan explained, "Mr. President, he has appeared twice now at the Dragon's Throat. He tried to carry off young Lila before, but we chased him away, and then he blew up the explosives in a supply shed."

The president sank into his couch again, but obviously he was not at all comfortable. "The Shaman has reappeared!"

"What do you know about this . . . this shaman?" Dr. Cooper wanted to know.

"He is a magician," said Gozan, "a powerful wizard!"

"He is a troublemaker!" the president countered. "A menace to this nation and to my plans! Upon the arrival of any expedition which intends to enter the Dragon's Throat, this elusive, scraggly little weasel comes out of hiding and makes himself out to be some kind of oracle, some kind of doom-sayer! He has threatened me with his warnings, and not only me but the entire country, trying to keep us from opening the Door!"

"And why haven't you arrested him?"

"He lives on the Street of the Scorpion!" Gozan answered.

Al-Dallam added glumly, "The Street of the Scorpion is a deadly trap for any outsider, especially our militia. It would be like searching for a deadly lion in the lion's own lair. There are hundreds of secret passages, back alleys, doorways, hiding places, and escape routes that only the Shaman knows. If we were to enter that maze, we would be playing right into his hands, and he could do whatever he wanted with us."

"Which is exactly what he's done with Jay and Lila," Dr. Cooper said.

"They are in grave danger," said Gozan. "We must . . . we must find them . . . somehow!"

At that very moment, Jay and Lila were huddled on a floor against a wall in a very small, dark, musty bungalow hidden deep within the intricate maze of winding streets, blind alleys, and obscure passageways. They were both looking up at what truly looked like a ghost: the dimly lit, ragged-robed, leathery-faced old man, the Shaman of the Desert. He stood there against the rough-hewn door trembling, the yellow light from a lone candle casting a slowly dancing shadow behind him.

Jay spoke first, and angrily. "All right, you've kidnapped us, you've thrown us in here, and I take it you're not going to let us go. Now what?"

The old man was blocking the door, but strangely enough he looked at least as afraid of Jay and Lila as they were of him.

With a low and trembling voice, he said, "Please . . . do not harm me. I mean you no evil."

Jay and Lila looked at each other quizzically. What kind of a kidnapper was this?

The old man's eyes were full of fear, and he almost seemed to be cowering against the door.

"Do not call a curse down upon me," he begged, "and may I find mercy in the eyes of your God. I must talk to you!"

Jay and Lila decided to play the game; so far it looked like they were winning.

"All right," said Jay, "what's on your mind?"

"I have seen that the God you serve is strong—indeed, strongest of all! I need your help!"

"Not so fast," Lila insisted. "Let's clear up the little matter of our supply shed and why you blew it up."

"I had to stop you. You . . . you must not open the Door. Believe me, it does not contain any treasure, but only evil."

Jay asked, "How do you know that?"

In answer to Jay's question, the old man moved slowly to a shelf, moved aside a thick blanket, and picked up a strange, black box. He brought it over to the table in the middle of the room and moved the candle closer.

"I," said the old man, "am the Keeper of the Sacred Chest."

"The Sacred Chest?" Lila questioned as she and Jay came over to the table.

The old man tilted the black chest toward them so they could have a better look at the lid.

"Well, will you look at that!" exclaimed Jay.

"The inscription!" Lila exclaimed. "It's the very same inscription as the one on the Door."

Jay could make out the familiar symbols. "The star that flew through heaven . . ."

The old man completed the sentence, pointing to the various symbols on the lid as he read them, ". . . will bring the key and all will be released."

"What is this box?" asked Jay. "What's in it?"

"According to our ancient traditions," said the old man, "it is the Sacred Chest of Shandago, the God of the Earth."

Jay asked again, "And what's in it?"

The old man hesitated before answering, as if he were about to reveal a very dark and forbidden secret. "According to the ancient traditions . . ." Again he hesitated. ". . . it holds the one and only key to the forbidden Door of Shandago!"

Jay and Lila looked at each other and read each other's face. They knew better than to betray any excitement, but this was a very, very intriguing discovery indeed.

"The Door of Shandago?" Jay asked.

"The Door in the Dragon's Throat!"

"And you have the key?" Lila asked.

"According to the ancient traditions, the Sacred Chest holds the key . . ."

"Don't you know for sure?" asked Jay.

"It is forbidden to open the Sacred Chest."

"You've never opened it?"

"Only Shandago, the God of the Earth, can open the Chest, and only at the proper time."

"Uh . . . just what kind of religion are you, anyway?" Lila asked.

The old man looked at them with tears in his eyes and explained, "I am . . . was . . . a Chaldean sorcerer, a wizard. All my ancestors and family were Chaldeans and magicians, well-versed in the ancient mystery religions of Babylon. For centuries we have worshiped the spirits of nature, the moon, the stars . . . and Shandago, the God of the Earth!" He looked down at the old black chest and ran his gnarled and leathery fingers over its surface as he said, "And we have been the Keepers of the Sacred Chest of Shandago. I received it from my father, who received if from his father, who received it from his father. From generation to generation, the keeping of the Sacred Chest has been passed down and entrusted to us."

Jay asked, "And are we to understand that you've never opened this thing, not even once?"

"It is forbidden for *anyone* to open it," the old man said, his eyes widening and glimmering in the candlelight. "We are not even to speak of it. My father . . ." His voice choked with a very deep-seated fear. "My father tried to open the Sacred Chest, and he died a horrible death! He did not learn from the death of *his* father, who also died horribly after *he* tried to open it."

"We're talking about a curse, in other words," said Lila.

"A curse that remains unbroken," said the old man. His eyes grew intense as he leaned forward and asked, "But your God is greater than any curse, yes? I have heard you speak such words, and you approached the Door and lived!"

"Well, He's certainly more than a match for this . . . this Shandago," said Jay. "But how does this god of yours fit into this? Are you saying that the Door was put there by your God of the Earth?"

The old man pointed to the inscription again. "He is the star! The star that fell from heaven!"

"Fell? I thought the word was 'flew.' "

"He is the star from heaven," the old man repeated. Then he lowered his voice and crouched low over the table to speak secrets to them. "I have been hounded by the spirit of your God! Listen to me—your God will not release me! He has followed me; He has spoken to my heart. He has opened my eyes, and now I see that Shandago is a liar."

The old man gave a little gasp, and his eyes darted about the room, full of fear that perhaps the pagan god he served had heard his words of betrayal. He continued whispering to them desperately. "This Sacred Chest . . . and the Door in the Dragon's Throat . . . and the God of the Earth—they are all unspeakably evil. Shandago has lied. He has fooled the people of Nepur into thinking the Door contains a vast treasure so they will try to open it, but it hides a terrible evil that he wishes to unleash upon the world. Please, I beg you, do not open the Door. Abandon any thought of it."

"Will you excuse us a minute?" Jay asked, pulling Lila aside.

The two of them huddled in a corner of the room and had a quick conference.

"What do you think?" Jay asked.

"I don't know about any of this. He's not making any sense."

"Well, he does make sense if you decipher what he's saying. Think of it, Lila. Nimrod was regarded as a deity by the ancient Babylonians, and they even believed that he became the sun and flew across the sky every day."

Lila's eyes brightened. "The star from heaven?"

"Exactly. All this fear and superstition is part of the old mysterious religions, sure, but clear all that away and what do you have?"

"The key to that lousy Door."

"*And* the treasure of Nimrod."

"So what do we do now?"

"Start praying and follow it through."

"Okay."

They broke their huddle and rejoined the old man at the table.

Jay asked, "What can we do to help you?"

The old man seemed relieved to hear Jay's offer. "The God you serve is greater than any other god, even the God of the Earth. I do not own this Chest—it owns *me!* Shandago rules my life and terrifies me with his curses, and now . . . since you have come and have brought your mighty God with you, I wonder . . ." The old man's eyes filled with tears, and he began to shake. "I wonder if your God could not make a way of escape for me, to free me from the curse of the Sacred Chest and from Shandago! Your God may have power over the curse that binds me."

Lila spoke gently. "His name is Jesus, and He does have power over this curse. He has power over any curse."

That was wonderful news to the trembling,

terrified shaman. "Then it is to this Jesus I must turn! Please, since you bear the name of Jesus, take the Sacred Chest. Destroy it and the curse! You can set me free!"

Lila leaned forward and spoke from her heart. "It sounds to me like you just need to be freed from your sin."

The old man nodded his head. "I have walked in darkness and fear all my life. My sins are like a chain about my heart."

"Listen," said Jay, putting his hand on the old man's shoulder, "you've just been working for the wrong god. Let us tell you about Jesus."

And they did. In that little bungalow, by the light of that one candle, Jay and Lila began to tell the old Chaldean sorcerer how to put aside his ancient occultic crafts and find true peace and forgiveness in Jesus. They had to put the gospel into pretty simple terms, but before long the old man began to understand that Jesus, the pure and holy Son of God, paid the price for sins with His own life so every person could be set free from sin, fear, and death, and could even be set free from any lying, evil gods that might be controlling his life.

With trembling hands clasped in fervent prayer, the old man wept and cried out, "I renounce the God of the Earth. I will no longer worship the sun, moon, and stars, nor the spirits of the dead. I now worship Jesus and His holy Father, the only true God."

Somehow the room seemed to suddenly be a

little brighter. The old man wept with joy as he looked heavenward, lifting his hands in joy and thanksgiving.

Outside the small window, unseen by the rejoicing saints inside, a silent, stealthy figure lurked in the darkness, watching and listening.

The old man drew a deep breath of air and smiled for the first time in years.

"I have just been born!" he proclaimed.

"Born again is the term Jesus used!" said Jay happily.

The old man clapped his hands as he laughed. "Yes, yes! I have begun to live again! The curse, the evil, is gone from my life!" Suddenly, as the thought returned to the ex-shaman, he grew very sober. "But the Door! The Door is still there! It must not be opened!" He grabbed the black box and shoved it into Jay's arms. "Here, please, you are strong in your God. Take the Chest and destroy it."

"Okay," said Jay. "But first I'm going to open it."

The old man's face paled with horror. "No! No! To open the Chest is to die!"

"Our God is greater, remember?"

"Yes, He is greater, but . . ."

"Don't worry," said Lila. "The Chest is harmless now."

"I'll be careful," Jay assured him. "But it's time this mysterious little box was opened."

The old man backed away from the table in a fear he couldn't help, but Jay took out his knife and began to carefully pry at the lid.

The old, dark wood was as hard as steel, and the lid was shut very tightly. Like the Door, it hadn't been opened in centuries. Jay stubbornly worked the sharp edge of the knife into the crack of the lid.

Just then the light in the room seemed to go dim.

Lila gasped. "What happened?"

"Relax," said Jay. "A cloud must have passed in front of the moon or something."

From the dark corner of the room came the voice of the cowering old man. "Jesus, You will protect us, yes?"

"He will."

Jay thought he had perhaps gotten a little bit of a crack started in one corner of the Chest. He worked from there, prying every few inches around the whole lid, ever widening the crack. Little bits of dirt and dust fell to the table.

Somewhere far-off along the Street of the Scorpion, a dog began to wail a long, mournful note.

Lila was getting edgy. "Jay, I think you'd better hurry."

"I don't want to damage this chest," he answered as he kept working slowly and methodically.

The crack grew wider under Jay's patient efforts, and eventually the lid began to raise from the chest.

"Just a little more now," said Jay.

He could hear the nervous breathing of the old man in the dark corner. The room seemed so dark.

"How's it going, Jay?" Lila asked, and now she was standing away from the table, watching from a distance.

"It's almost off," he answered.

He pried some more with the blade, and the lid loosened, then moved upward easily. It came up a little more, and a little more.

Then it came off.

The room filled with an old, musty smell, as if a tomb had just been opened. Fine, gray dust fell in little puffs from the lid as Jay set it down on the table. The Chest seemed to be filled with it. Jay took a spoon and probed the gray surface. He found a piece of cloth, now totally decayed and crumbling, and moved it aside. It crumbled into powder. He carefully removed that powder and the fine little shreds that were left.

Lila came up to the table for a closer look and had to sneeze some of the gray dust out of her nose. Finally the old man also stepped very timidly up to the table, and the three of them peered down into the Chest.

Jay took the spoon and began to carefully scoop out the gray dust and the rotted shreds of cloth wrapping. After just a few scoops, the spoon clunked against something metal.

"Oh, oh," said Jay.

He reached in, very gently took hold of whatever it was, and lifted it slowly up and out. The dust fell away from the object in little lumps. The smell was musty and horrible.

"Bingo . . . I think," said Lila.

"I am seeing it," said the old man. "I am seeing it with my own eyes."

Jay blew the dust away and wiped the object with an old rag. The more he wiped it, the shinier it got, until they could see that it was made of beautiful, glimmering, bronzelike metal.

Lila observed, "It's the same metal the Door is made of!"

"Will you look at that!" said Jay, holding it up, turning it this way and that, trying to figure it out.

The metal object looked like some strange alien garden tool—with a handle at one end, a long narrow shaft, and then a strange, clawlike cluster of fingers at the other end.

Jay thought he'd figured it out. "Remember the shape of that keyhole in the Door? You hold this end, and then this end here—with all these fingers on it—goes into that lock, and there you are!"

"The key to the Door of Shandago!" exclaimed the old man.

"Or Nimrod," added Jay.

Suddenly a cold wind caressed their necks, making the hair on their necks bristle. Outside more dogs were mourning and howling, their moans and cries filtering down through the narrow streets and alleys.

"I am afraid," said the old man.

Jay didn't hear his comment; he was too interested in his theory about the key. "Sure, it makes sense. The ancient Chaldeans got their mystery religion and beliefs from Babylon, from Nimrod. Obviously, when Nimrod passed down his religion to the Chaldeans, he also entrusted them with the key to his treasure. The keeping of the key became part of their religion."

"There is more," said the old man, his eyes wide with fear as he looked around the room and out the windows. "I can feel it. Evil is at work tonight."

The cold wind raced in through the window again and chilled them with icy fingers of air. The candle flickered.

"Lila, see if you can close the shutter there."

Lila took only a few steps toward the window and then screamed.

"What!" cried Jay, racing to her side.

"There was someone out there!" she gasped.

The old man was immediately there too, looking out the window.

"I see no one," he said.

"I saw someone!" Lila insisted. "Someone in a wide-brimmed hat. He was right at the window."

The three of them peered up and down the narrow street, but saw no one.

"Well, he's gone now," said Jay.

They turned back inside.

The old man gasped. He fell backward against the wall, his hand over his heart, his eyes filled with terror.

Jay and Lila looked in the direction of his terrified gaze.

The heavy door stood open as the cold night wind entered and raced about the room, raising the hairs on their arms and teasing the candle flame. The table in the middle of the room still had the old, open chest upon it.

But the key—the key to the Door—was gone.

# SIX

Jay bolted for the door and got as far as the street outside before the old man locked onto his arm with a viselike grip.

"Let me go!" Jay shouted. "He has the key!"

"No! No!" the old man insisted. "Not on the Street of the Scorpion. You will never find him, but will become lost, and then *he* will find *you!*"

"But he has the key."

"He also has the curse."

"There isn't any curse."

"Oh no?"

Suddenly there came a terrible crash of thunder and a cold blast of angry wind. The moon disappeared behind a boiling curtain of inky black clouds, and dogs all over the city began to howl and bark. From somewhere came a scream, and then another, and then the nerve-chilling shriek of a cat.

"We must find your father," said the old man.

"We must explain everything to him. I'll show you the way back."

The three of them started out through the terrible darkness, hurrying along the maze of narrow streets and alleys. Jay and Lila had no idea where they were going, but the old man seemed to know every turn, every doorway, every narrow passage. He raced along, towing them by the hand, ducking, running, leaping through doorways, under walls, along narrow ledges. They jumped from rooftop to rooftop and climbed up and down long, precarious stairways.

The clouds above them continued to boil and churn. Suddenly, frightening in their startling, night-shattering brillance, huge bolts of lightning split the sky, accompanied by teeth-rattling thunder.

The old man ran and ran, pulling Jay and Lila along with him. They came to a wall with an old stone stairway leading upward and a very narrow tunnel going downward.

"The stairs would be the safest," he said, "but the tunnel would be the quickest."

"We'll take the tunnel," said Jay.

Lila didn't have time to offer her opinion before the three of them ducked down into the narrow hole. They soon found themselves sliding on their behinds down a slick and slimy storm drain which dropped past many old stone foundations, drain outlets, and side tunnels. They finally came to a stop on the floor of a subterranean vault, scaring hundreds of cat-sized rats into hiding. Jay's flashlight beam caught the gleaming white faces of countless skulls grinning at them from the walls.

"A burial vault?" he asked.

"This place is taboo, but a very good thoroughfare if one is freed from curses," said the old man.

The three hurried along, ducking under low beams and cutting around sharp corners, their feet splashing through large pools of black, rancid water. Thick, tangled spiderwebs wrapped around their faces with disgusting regularity, but they pulled them off and kept going.

At last, after squeezing through a very tight space between two stone walls, they came upon a well shaft that went down into eerie blackness, but also soared high above them. Water trickled down its sides while flashes of lightning flickered across the opening and reflected down the wet walls, lighting the shaft with spooky blue rays.

The old man started climbing a long series of primitive hand- and footholds made of stone, and Jay and Lila followed him. Every step was slippery, and they hung on sometimes only by their fingernails, desperate for a good grip on anything. Below them, the deep well shaft disappeared into blackness, and they could hear the heavily echoed trickling of water.

Lila suddenly slipped. She grabbed Jay's foot just above her as her own feet dangled helplessly above the abyss. The old man held Jay firmly until Lila could place her feet in the slippery cavities once again. They then continued their long, vertical climb.

They could hear the echo of the wind howling

down the well, and flashes of lightning came fast and furious. The wind whipped downward into the shaft and spit cold spray in their faces.

Finally, with a few last desperate clawings at the slippery stones, they emerged from the shaft and found themselves in a wide, deserted street. All around them, the windows were tightly shuttered; there was no sign of life anywhere. The clouds above still boiled angrily, and the lightning was terrifyingly close. The old man looked all around, his face etched with fear.

"Please," he said over the rush of the cold wind, "we must call on the name of Jesus and His Father our God. Evil is rampant in the city tonight. Perhaps we have brought it upon ourselves."

A sharp flash of light suddenly surrounded them. The entire street lit up with an intense glow, and they fell to the ground.

"Jay!" a familiar, booming voice called. "Lila!"

It was their father! The light came from the headlights of his jeep.

"Dad!" they cried. They ran to him as he leaped from the jeep and embraced them.

"Are you all right?" he asked.

"Just fine," said Jay.

"Boy, have we got something to tell you!" Lila piped in.

Dr. Cooper noticed the old ex-shaman standing there, and his muscles tensed.

"Who is this man?" he said coldly.

Jay tried to reassure him. "A friend, Dad. A

friend who means well—and a new believer in Jesus!"

Still feeling some reservation, Dr. Cooper offered his hand to the former kidnapper. "I am Dr. Cooper . . ."

"Yes, yes," the old man replied, taking Dr. Cooper's hand. "The children's father!"

"Everybody into the jeep," said Dr. Cooper. "We've got to get back to the president's palace. I've discovered something important to all of us."

They clambered into the jeep and Lila said, "So have we, Dad."

As the jeep roared out of the east side of the city and back toward the affluent section of town, Jay and Lila told Dr. Cooper everything that had happened, especially about their discovery of the one and only key and about the mysterious thief who had stolen it.

Dr. Cooper listened raptly, then said, "Jay and Lila, you don't know how serious this is. We must find that key. We must get the president to help us, even if it takes the whole Nepurian army."

The jeep roared up in front of the magnificent presidential palace, and the four of them ran down the huge marble halls, then burst through the big teakwood doors and into the president's office.

The president was gone!

"Where is he?" Dr. Cooper asked no one in particular, looking every which way for any sign of the man. "I just left him here before I went to find you. We must speak with him."

Dr. Cooper grabbed the telephone from the president's desk. The line was dead, but he noted that the receiver was picking up strange, rumbling noises.

Thunder crashed outside, and the wind started screaming and wailing past the windows, rattling the panes and making the roof beams groan. The limbs of trees slapped loudly against the building.

He slammed down the telephone and announced, "We'll have to search the building."

"That won't be necessary," a gruff voice behind them said.

They turned toward the door, and there stood Gozan, grinning his big yellow grin and pointing a gun at them.

"Hands up, hands up!" he ordered, and they all complied. "Dr. Cooper, you may drop your weapon."

Dr. Cooper reached slowly into his holster and pulled out his gun. He set it down carefully on the floor.

"Gozan," he asked with a steady voice, "where is the president?"

Gozan just kept smirking, a picture of arrogance. "No need for you to know, good doctor. He did give me my orders, though. He told me I am to . . . *take care* of you!"

Gozan seemed very cocky, but Dr. Cooper noticed that his hands were shaking.

"Gozan, are you afraid of something?"

The hand holding the gun shook even more, maybe dangerously so, as Gozan yelled angrily,

"Don't try to play games with me, Dr. Cooper! I am in charge now!" Then he relaxed his voice a little and went back to his arrogant smirk. "You would not think to share the great treasure of Nimrod with me. So now . . . I will not think to share it with you."

Suddenly Lila noticed Gozan's very familiar, wide-brimmed hat. "You're the thief who was outside the window!"

Gozan laughed his fiendish laugh. "You are very observant, Miss Lila. Yes, it was me. I knew where to find the old shaman, and I overheard everything you said about the wonderful, magical key."

Dr. Cooper could no longer stand still. He took a step forward, and Gozan pointed the gun at him threateningly.

"Gozan," Dr. Cooper said earnestly, "you must give us that key. You must not try to open the Door."

"Doctor, don't tell me what to do. I am in control now. We have the key, and we will be able to open the Door without you. You are no longer needed."

Dr. Cooper was looking at Gozan's hands again. "Gozan, you *are* afraid. I can see it."

Gozan screamed his denial. "I am not afraid!"

"Listen to me. Listen, Gozan. There is *no* treasure."

A streak of lightning flashed across the sky, and thunder rattled the whole building. The lights began to blink on and off. Gozan stood there, his eyes darting to and fro; sweat ran down his face.

Dr. Cooper kept pounding away at him. "Did you hear me, Gozan? There is no treasure. We were wrong about the Door."

Gozan almost sounded desperate as he cried, "I don't believe you."

"Everything you feared about the Door is true. The Door is evil."

"The Door is evil," the old man agreed.

Jay was surprised at what his father was saying. "Dad, what are you talking about?"

Dr. Cooper glanced sideways at Jay as he spoke, keeping one eye on the barrel of Gozan's gun. "We had the legend figured out all wrong, Jay. I misread the inscription. The star didn't *fly through* heaven; it *fell from* heaven!"

"That's . . . that's . . ."

"That is what *I* said," said the old man.

Dr. Cooper continued, "Think about it. The star that fell from heaven. Where have you heard that phrase before?"

Gozan protested, "You . . . you said it was Nimrod, the great Babylonian king."

"The term also applies to someone else. I found it today, in the Bible. I knew I'd read it somewhere before."

Jay was pleading now. "Where, Dad? What does it say?"

Dr. Cooper spoke slowly and deliberately. "Revelation, chapter 9. A star fallen from heaven to earth. Those exact words!"

Jay began to recall that passage. "Yeah . . . that's right."

They all felt a shuddering, a rumble from

deep under the floor. The chandeliers began to sway back and forth.

"Here we go again," said Lila.

"It is the evil," said the old man. "It is the Door."

Gozan began to tremble and gasp for breath. "I don't believe you! You are trying to trick me!"

Dr. Cooper wouldn't let him relax, but kept speaking in earnest. "Oh, I am, huh? Remember, Gozan? Remember how the earth would shake every time we got near the Door? Remember what happened to all the other expeditions? How they died, went crazy, ran in terror? Remember how nothing would grow anywhere around the Dragon's Throat?"

Gozan's eyes were huge with fright. He struggled to stand on his feet. His fear was nearly more than he could stand.

"The Door does not belong to Nimrod!" Dr. Cooper insisted. "Nimrod didn't put it there. Someone else did."

Jay was dying to know. "Who, Dad? Who?"

"Put it together, Jay. The star that fell from heaven . . . the God of the Earth . . . and that name the old man used: Shandago. That's an old expression for the word dragon or serpent. Those terms are in the Bible."

The truth hit Jay and Lila. The old man already knew it, but in different terms.

Jay said it in horror. "Satan!"

Dr. Cooper pointed his finger right at Gozan, and it could have been a gun, the effect on the poor trembling man was so severe. "Gozan, we've got to have that key! You must not open the Door!"

"No . . . no . . ." Gozan pleaded in a higher and higher voice.

"That rumbling we heard, that strange humming like a beehive . . . remember that?" Dr. Cooper's eyes burned like fire as he pronounced the horrible truth to this wilting bandit. "There are *demons* behind that Door, Gozan, countless demons specially appointed to torture and destroy mankind. They've been waiting thousands of years to be let out of there. You must give us that key!"

The words grated and scratched their way out of Gozan's trembling jaws one by one. "I . . . I do not have the key . . . !"

"Where is it, Gozan?"

"I . . . I gave it to the president. He has gone to the Dragon's Throat . . ." Gozan was obviously terrified by his own words. "He is going . . . to open the Door!"

# SEVEN

As if to acknowledge the horrible news Gozan had just revealed, another bolt of lightning zigzagged down from the sky and exploded in a ball of white light right outside the window, sizzling in the trees and breaking several panes of glass.

Gozan covered his head with his arms and screamed, "The curse! The curse! We are bringing the curse upon us!"

The earth continued to reel and shake, and the chandeliers were now slapping and tinkling against the ceiling.

"We can help, Gozan," Dr. Cooper shouted. "You must let us help you."

Gozan stumbled to his knees from the shaking and began to grovel pitifully. "You . . . you all bear the name of Jesus. Can you save us from the evil?"

"If we don't act immediately it will be too late! Put down the gun!"

Gozan looked around, wild-eyed, at the storm

crashing and roaring outside the broken windows, at the swinging chandeliers and the blinking lights, at the rocking and swaying of the building. Finally he slowly began to lower the gun, his white-knuckled hand too shaky to aim accurately at anything anyway.

"Yes, that's it . . ." Dr. Cooper urged him, moving forward just a little.

But then the tremors began to subside, the lights came on again, and Gozan regained his nerve. The gun raised once more, with its barrel pointed right at Dr. Cooper. Dr. Cooper froze. Gozan smiled fiendishly.

But without warning, another tremor hit, and another bolt of lightning exploded just outside the palace. The lights blinked; the wind roared.

Gozan had had enough. He threw the gun aside. "I surrender! I surrender!"

There was no time for discussion. The Coopers and the old man dashed past Gozan's fallen form and ran out the door.

Gozan curled up tightly on the floor, covering his head with his arms and cowering. "Jesus, great God, please save us!" he pled.

The four hurried, staggering their way down the rocking, reeling marble hallway to the big front doors that were now swinging and slamming wildly. The wind carried sticks, leaves, papers, and streaks of rain in a fierce, sideways torrent that almost knocked them over as they ran for the jeep.

Dr. Cooper cranked the engine over, put the old vehicle into gear, and floored the gas pedal.

The jeep's rear wheels dug into the ground and sent out a spray of rocks and dirt as the jeep fishtailed this way and that and roared out through the palace gates. They sped past shops, stores, and frightened, cowering citizens, the engine screaming in desperation. They slid around a corner and took the road that led out toward the desert, toward the Dragon's Throat.

Jay pointed to the desert horizon, but they had all seen it. A hellish, red glow flickered there, as if a terrible fire were burning in the desert, rising and falling, a red and pink arc reaching into the night sky, nearly washing out the stars.

The awesome scene reminded them all of the terrible words of Revelation, chapter 9.

"I saw a star fallen from heaven to earth, and he was given the key of the shaft of the bottomless pit; he opened the shaft of the bottomless pit, and from the shaft rose smoke like the smoke of a great furnace, and the sun and the air were darkened with the smoke from the shaft. Then from the smoke came locusts on the earth, and they were given power like the power of scorpions of the earth. . . . their torture was like the torture of a scorpion, when it stings a man. And in those days men will seek death and will not find it; they will long to die, and death will fly from them."

Demons were captive in the Dragon's Throat! Demons as thick as locusts, so many millions of them that they would appear as a cloud of smoke, all reserved for terrible judgment upon the world, all hidden and waiting for eons of time deep within the earth, deep within the bottomless pit, the great prison sealed shut by the great Door in the Dragon's Throat!

The Coopers really had no idea what they would do or what they *could* do, but Dr. Cooper kept driving across the desert, jerking the steering wheel violently to keep the jeep on the rolling, quaking roadway. The towering rock formations all around them were swaying and crumbling. Perhaps even more dangerous, huge pieces of rock were coming down like missiles and blasting great holes in the roadway, first here, then there, in front, behind, alongside. Dr. Cooper swerved to dodge them as the jeep traced a crazy path.

Up one hill, down the next, winding, turning, racing along, all four of the wide-eyed saints kept praying a mile a minute, even shouting their prayers out loud.

"Lord God, get us there in time! We plead the blood of Jesus to protect us and conquer this thing!"

They came to the last hill. When Dr. Cooper gunned the jeep, it dug and clawed its way up to the crest and then, like a pouncing cat, dove over the top of the hill as they all lifted out of their seats.

They all saw it. Dr. Cooper kept driving pell-mell down the hill into the valley, but they all saw it and couldn't take their eyes off it.

The Dragon's Throat had come alive with a hideous, crimson glow, the entire barren circle reflecting the red, pulsating light now coming from the pit like an immense, mirror-smooth pool of blood. The boiling clouds in the sky were washed with the reddish tint as they churned like an inverted caldron, and the terrified four could hear the howling roar rushing up out of the pit, so loud they could hear it from this distance, even over the roar of the jeep.

Closer and closer they came, their faces illuminated with the fiery red light, their hands tightly gripping the bucking jeep. At last the jeep bounded into the forbidden circle and raced to the camp at the edge of the pit, skidding sideways in a cloud of firelit dust. They piled out onto the quaking ground and crouched behind the jeep for protection. It was like standing at the edge of an erupting volcano.

The camp was a shambles. The tents were collapsed and shredded, the supply sheds blown over and splintered, the equipment shattered and tossed about like litter. Jeff, Tom, and Bill were nowhere to be seen and apparently had fled.

But across the Dragon's Throat, parked right at the edge, near the stairway, was the president's limousine.

"He's here, all right!" Dr. Cooper shouted to the others.

Overwhelmed with a sense of danger, they nevertheless came out from behind the jeep and ran around the edge of the cavern until they could reach the limousine. It was empty. They could see footprints of the president's chauffeur leading over the hill; the spacing of the prints indicated he'd run like a madman. As for the president's tracks, they led right to the stairway. He was down below at that very moment.

Jay shouted over the roar of the wind and the howl of the Dragon's Throat, "What now?"

Dr. Cooper huddled close and shouted, "We've no choice. We'll have to go down after him. We'll have to face this thing." He shouted to the old man, "You may flee to safety and wait for us if you wish."

The old man was very shaken with fear and nodded in agreement. "It would be best. I can remain above and pray to our God." He embraced them quickly and then ran out into the desert to a safer distance.

Dr. Cooper, followed by Jay and Lila, came to the edge and looked down into a very dizzying, horrifying whirlwind of red, glowing smoke and dust that rushed and rose around and around the walls of the Dragon's Throat like a cyclone. The Dragon's Throat could not have been better named, and now it seemed eager to swallow them up.

The stairway was strongly built and had managed to survive so far. They went to it and grabbed the railing, taking one step downward at a time, facing the wall, hanging on for dear life, the roaring wind ripping at their clothing and hair, the dust and debris stinging their skin like hail.

Down one step, then another, then another. Sometimes the wind would whip them around sideways and slam them into the rocks. They clung to the railing and each other, working their way down, down into the heart of the cavern. The Dragon's Throat almost seemed to be breathing. The wind rushed in pulses, first fierce and hot, then less severe; then another blast of wind would swirl from below and nearly scorch them.

"Dad," Lila screamed, "we'll never make it!"

"Our God is greater!" was Dr. Cooper's quick reply. "We have no choice. We have to try."

As the descent became more gradual, they were able to make better time, and finally reached the floor of the cavern.

Now they could look up and see the glowing gases flowing in a torrent like an upside-down river just above their heads, rippling and roaring along the ceiling of the corridor. They ducked down close to the sandy floor and ran deeper into the cavern, steadying themselves against the rock walls to keep from pitching over as the earth continued to quake and lurch.

They began to call out, "Mr. President! Mr. President, where are you?" But there was no answer.

As they crouched and scurried along, the "river" above them gave them the dizzying illusion that they were rushing along at great speed. They had to keep their hands on the walls to keep steady.

Then they came to the main room.

They immediately dropped to the floor, taking cover.

"Our God is greater!" Jay screamed, mostly to remind himself.

Never had they seen anything quite so frightening. The Door could be seen at the far end of the room, looking like the sun during a total eclipse. The face of the Door was dark, maybe glowing a dull pink, but all around its edges was a brilliant red light, the rays shooting out in all directions and projecting solid, undulating curtains of red through the smoke and haze that filled the room. Black vapor seeped out through the cracks in thin, curling sheets, and the Door was creaking, rumbling, groaning, moving with a deafening roar like that of a million giant hornets echoing and reverberating behind it. The Door seemed to be breathing, heaving in and out, though actually it was being pushed from behind, inch by inch, as some incredible force was steadily, relentlessly pushing it open.

Dr. Cooper shouted to the kids, "We've got to find that key! Look at the keyhole!"

They could see a sharp, laserlike beam of red shooting out from the keyhole in the Door and sweeping about the room like the beam from a lighthouse.

"The Door has been unlocked!" Dr. Cooper explained. "We must find the key! The lock may be reversible!"

They scurried from their hiding places on the floor and fanned out to search the room. Dr. Cooper took one side, Jay the other, and Lila went up the middle. They began to search for the president by the light of the glowing, roaring Door itself.

The Door groaned again, inching forward even further.

Lila ran among the rocky formations and fallen boulders, looking here and there, calling for the president. She could hear her father and brother doing the same. All three of them worked their way across the room, getting closer and closer to that menacing Door, feeling the heat from it more and more.

Lila crawled over a rocky crag and down the other side and suddenly tumbled down right on top of the president. He sat with his back against the rocks, his mouth gaping, his eyes wide in trancelike shock. He was motionless, staring at the Door.

"Jay! Dad! Over here!"

Jay and Dr. Cooper were there immediately.

Dr. Cooper stooped down and shook the fear-crazed man. "Mr. President! Mr. President!"

For a moment they couldn't tell if he was dead or alive.

"He's in shock," said Jay.

"Quite so, and worse!" said Dr. Cooper.

There was a loud, nerve-chilling, metallic groan that echoed through the big room. The Door was inching further forward, and they could all feel a new wave of heat.

Then Jay saw it. "Dad! In his hand!"

It was the key. The president's hand was curled tightly around it. Jay reached down to take it, but the hand was clenched in an iron grip of terror.

"Please, Mr. President," he said, "please let me have the key."

They tried to uncurl his fingers one by one.

"C'mon . . . c'mon . . ."

Suddenly, with a bloodcurdling scream, the president came up off the ground like an explosion, sending them all tumbling. He took one crazy-eyed look at the Door, screamed, "They're coming out, they're coming out," and ran like a madman, in circles, up and down formations, bumping into rocks, screaming and struggling to escape.

"After him!" Dr. Cooper yelled. "Mr. President, come back!"

They tried to catch him, but his direction was totally unpredictable. Like a crazed animal, he clambered up a rocky wall of the cavern, going higher and higher, jumping from this ledge to that, falling, climbing up again, scratching, clawing, grabbing the rocks, gasping in fright. The Coopers followed him, tried to call to him, but he was deaf to their voices. He reached a high, perilous ledge and then hesitated, trapped, unable to go any further.

Dr. Cooper yelled, "Mr. President, it's Dr. Cooper, Jay, Lila! We're here to help you! Do you understand?"

"They're coming out!" he screamed, turning in wild, crazy circles on the ledge.

The Coopers started up after him, but it was too late. Suddenly another terrible tremor of the earth shook the cavern. The rocks quivered, began to roll and slide, and the Coopers had to leap for cover.

There was a long, terrible scream, and Jay looked just in time to see the president go tumbling off the ledge, tumbling over and over until he disappeared into a deep crevasse. In the red glow of the Door, Jay could see the twinkling, spinning reflection of light off the key as it flew through the air, bounced off some rocks, flipped several more times from rock to rock with a metallic ring, and finally sailed into the crevasse and out of sight.

"No, Lord God, no!" he cried.

They all ran to the edge and saw that miraculously there was still hope. The key had landed on a narrow ledge some eight feet down and was balanced there precariously, tilting, teeter-tottering over the abyss.

The Door shook, belched out more smoke, and slid forward yet another fraction of an inch.

Dr. Cooper hollered, "Lila, you first!"

She crawled headfirst down into the crevasse as Jay grabbed her ankles. Jay followed right after her as the second link in the chain, and Dr. Cooper anchored his body between some rocks and took hold of Jay's ankles.

Lila reached for the key, strained to grab it, but just wasn't close enough.

Dr. Cooper slid forward, lowering Jay and Lila further into the abyss. Lila reached for the key again, but still could not quite reach it.

The big room was filled with a loud, fierce pounding as the Door seemed to ripple with the impact of terrific forces ramming it from behind. The very edges of the Door were becoming visible as it inched forward.

Dr. Cooper held on with all his strength, praying desperately. The earth shook fiercely, knocking Lila around in the abyss like a rag doll. The key began to tilt toward the edge, then slid a little. Lila was still swinging about, but then she made use of her movement, pushed herself off one wall of the crevasse, and swung over near the key. She reached out with straining fingertips to grasp the key.

She got it!

"Pull me up!" she screamed. "Pull me up!"

Dr. Cooper strained and pulled against the rocks to back away from the edge, and finally worked Jay up out of the crevasse. Then the two of them snatched Lila out of the jaws of the abyss. They scurried down the rocky walls to the cavern floor.

Boulders were falling all around them. The ceiling was breaking up! They dashed for cover, Dr. Cooper and Lila darting toward the back of the room, Jay finding no other way to go but toward the Door. With a tremendous rumble and roar, a whole section of the ceiling fell, and instantly there was a mountain of rubble in the middle of the room, a huge wall that separated Jay from his family.

One sizable rock bounced wildly, spun crazily through the air, punched several dents in the floor, and then caught Dr. Cooper from behind, pinning him down.

"Dad!" Lila cried out.

Dr. Cooper looked at the suddenly formed wall of rock and knew Jay was on the other side.

"Jay!" he shouted.

"I'm all right!" came the answer.

Dr. Cooper looked across the room at Lila, who was still trying to hide from the falling rocks.

"Lila!" he called. "The key!"

She threw the key with all her might. It tumbled through the air and plinked down next to her father. He grabbed it, hollered, "Jay!" and then hurled the key up and over the rock wall.

It came down in a high, spinning arc, dashed against one rock, flipped several times through the air, plinked and bounced down several more rocks, and then landed with a puff of dust on the floor. Jay was there immediately to snatch it up, and then turned to face the Door.

The Door was groaning metallically, heaving, quaking, glowing red hot. The cracks all around it were widening, widening, widening. Red light beamed out all around it, and smoke and vapor poured out into the room. From behind it came the sound of a hurricane. Suddenly Jay felt very small, a tiny ant before the horrible, towering monster now advancing toward him. For a moment he could feel himself being paralyzed with panic; he even thought his heart had stopped.

Then his father's voice came from the other side of the rocks: "Jay, rebuke it! Turn them back!"

Wake up, Jay, wake up! he thought to himself. He held the key in a trembling, outstretched arm and spoke to the Door.

"I come against you in the name of Jesus!" he cried. "And I command you to get back in there!"

As if in response, the earth shook violently, throwing Jay to the ground. The Door quivered and vibrated as incredible forces kept ramming it from behind. But suddenly a new sound emerged, a sound like a million sirens, wailing, crying, shrieking in ear-jarring pitches that rose and fell. Something had happened!

Jay spoke again. "In the name of Jesus I command you to get back in there!"

The sirens and screams grew louder. The Door kept groaning and quivering, but . . . had it stopped advancing?

Jay grabbed his chance. He dashed for the scaffold built against the Door and began scrambling up rung after rung, pulling with all the strength his arms could muster, pushing and propelling himself with his legs. Ten feet, twenty feet, thirty feet, forty feet—up the scaffold he went.

He reached the top level, more than fifty feet above the cavern floor, and here the scaffold swayed like a palm tree in a hurricane. He carefully crawled along the rough planks, hanging on to anything his hands could find. He was in the thick of the smoke and vapor, and he couldn't breathe. The red fire seemed to be all around him. The scaffold was quivering, shaking, swaying, creaking. He was afraid he would fall at any moment.

Now he was right beside the glowing, angry surface of the Door. He could see it shaking, moving, pressing against the scaffold. He could hear the roar of the spirits behind it.

Where is the keyhole? Where is the keyhole? Dear God, show me where it is! he prayed desperately.

There! That brilliant beam of light! Jay

crawled toward it, inching forward, hanging on precariously. The plank next to him shuddered and slid off the scaffold, dropping end over end to the cavern floor, where it shattered and splintered on the rocks.

The keyhole was right over Jay's head now. He worked his way up to a kneeling position, took hold of the key firmly, and began to fumble around the hole with it, trying to find the right fit, the right angle. He turned the key, twisted it. The fingers of the key bounced and clanged against the hot metal, and finally went in. He let go for only a moment, so he could get a better grip.

Something shoved the key back out of the hole! Jay grabbed it just in time and jammed it back in again. He could feel the pressure from the other side. He was in a push-of-war!

"Stop!" he yelled.

Through the keyhole he could hear screams, the roar of wings, the hissing of nostrils. Never had he been in such direct conflict with the enemy powers.

Just as he started to turn the key, his legs dropped from under him. The scaffold was collapsing! He clung to the key desperately as the timbers, the planks, the nails, the nuts and bolts all crumbled like a house of cards and dropped, seemingly in slow motion, to the rocks below, where they flew apart like shattering glass.

The Door had pushed the scaffold over!

I'm going to die, thought Jay. These demons know I'm here, and they want to kill me!

But he refused to let go. Fifty feet up, he

hung onto that key, still stuck in the hole. Then, working one hand at a time, he began to twist the key with the weight of his dangling body, one turn, one more turn, grip by painful grip, inch by inch.

The Door seemed to know what he was doing. It shook, it heaved, it quaked, and Jay's body was tossed and whipped about as he hung onto the key. His legs and chest slapped against the hot bronze metal of the Door, and he could feel the searing heat scorch his clothes and singe his skin. Terrible pain poured over his body and shot through his aching arms.

He managed another turn of the key, then another. The screams behind the Door grew louder. He could feel vibrations and jarrings through the handle of the key.

He could hardly catch enough breath to say, "Lord Jesus, help me!"

The earth shook again, and Jay's body was flung to and fro. He knew he couldn't hold on much longer.

And then, above all the other sounds, came a very loud cracking. Jay turned his head just in time to see a section of the opposite wall shear off, pitch forward, tumble down the incline to the cavern floor, and start rolling right toward him.

He heaved on the key and gave it half a turn, then looked again. The huge chunk of rock was still rolling, end over end, crunching and crushing, bounding and bouncing, closer and closer. It was the size of a house.

Another half a turn. Jay could hear metal

moving inside the lock. The boulder was coming in like a roaring tide, faster and faster.

Suddenly the lock was vibrating. Something was falling into place.

One more turn on the key!

The boulder, with all its multiplied tons of mass, moving at incredible speed, flopped and rolled and crunched its way across the cavern floor.

One more turn!

A thunderous crash echoed many times throughout the huge cave. Fire and smoke shot out from all around the Door as it flexed violently in the middle, shuddered, groaned, and lurched backward. The edges shrieked metallically, sending out showers of sparks as they ground back into the wall. The screams from inside were suddenly cut off.

As for Jay, the impact was so great and so sudden that he had no time to even be aware of it. All at once the key that had been in his hands was no longer there; the Door itself was suddenly several feet away from him. He was falling . . . falling . . . falling . . .

Silence. Blackness. No more pain.

"Jay . . ." came a very distant voice. "Jay . . ."

It was dark. It was cold. From somewhere Jay saw a light.

"Jay . . . son, can you hear me?"

Jay's eyes slowly began to focus. The light . . . a flashlight. He recognized his father's voice.

"Jay?"

"Dad?"

"Yes!" The voice sounded relieved. "We're both here, Dad and Lila."

Jay raised his head and looked. Yes, he saw them both. They were smiling.

Dr. Cooper said, "You did it, son. You and the Lord."

Jay sat up slowly. He was hurting all over; his leg felt numb and detached.

"Steady there," said his father. "It's a little precarious up here."

Dr. Cooper shined his flashlight around so Jay could see that the three of them were perched on top of a tremendously huge boulder. The flashlight beam moved another direction, and there was the bronze surface of that infernal Door! The boulder was resting against it; the Door was cold and dark. The whole cavern was dead quiet.

"You have to hand it to the Lord, son," said Dr. Cooper. "He has terrific timing. If this boulder hadn't rolled underneath you, you would have fallen all the way to the bottom. I've checked your leg. It looks like a bad sprain, but no breaks."

"Yeah . . ." Jay said, wincing in pain. "I remember . . . I remember seeing this boulder coming at the Door . . ."

"It was quite a collision . . . and it did the trick. The Door is shut, and the lock is in place again, thanks to you. It's a real miracle."

Jay looked up. He could see the keyhole. Now it seemed so high above him. But the key, the mysterious key, was gone.

"What happened to the key?"

Dr. Cooper answered, "Lost, I suppose. Gone without a trace. But when the time is right for God's Word to be fulfilled . . . when the *Lord* wants it to happen, no doubt old Satan will get his chance at last. He'll bring the key, and he'll open the Door."

The thought of that was awesome. "And all this will start happening all over again?" Jay moaned.

"And with no interruptions. But don't worry. If I understand the Bible correctly, we won't be around to see it. The Lord will get us out of here before then."

Jay looked at the Door. It seemed so cold, dark, and lifeless now.

"I think," he said, "I'd like to get out of here right *now!*"

"I'm with you," said Lila.

Dr. Cooper and Lila carefully helped Jay get up, and with great care they all climbed down from the huge boulder. They limped and walked out of the big room and at length emerged, torn, tattered, but triumphant, from the Dragon's Throat, leaving it behind forever.


Someday the end of history will come. Someday Satan will have his very short time of unleashed evil and destruction upon mankind. But now, then, and always, there is only one great power truly in charge: Jesus, the Victor, the Lamb, the Son of the Living God.